Second Chances at Channel View Farm

Channel View Series

(A Fabrian Books' Feel-Good Novel)

Jo Bartlett

Typesetting and Design Fabrian Books – fabrianbooks.com.

About the Author

Jo writes romance and women's fiction in the pockets of time she finds between her day jobs, as a leadership writer and university lecturer, and family life. Jo lives with her husband, four children and four dogs on the Kent coast, so far to the south east of England that they're very nearly French.

Jo is one tenth of the Write Romantics, and is published by Fabrian Books, So Vain Books, DC Thomson, Ulverscoft, Oakhill Press and Recorded Books, and still can't quite believe she's had nine books published. It took a brush with cancer to finally make Jo take the time to sit down and write that first book and it's now her biggest ambition to drink tea and make stuff up on a full time basis.

You can find out more about Jo at:

www.jobartlettauthor.com

Other books by this author

The St Nicholas Bay Series

Somebody Else's Boy
The Gift of Christmas Yet to Come
A Song for St Nicholas

Fabrian Books' Feel-Good Novels

A Holly Bay Christmas
The Christmas Shop at Central Park
A Highland Practice

The Channel View Farm Series

Give Me Your Answer Do

So Vain Books

Among A Thousand Stars

For the Joneses, how every family should be

XX

Chapter One

"Grey skies. Typical!" The woman sitting to the left of Olivia looked out of the window and then turned back towards her, pulling a face as the pilot announced their descent into Heathrow. "Don't you wish you could just get off the plane and get straight back on the next one to Australia?"

"Honestly, no, I can't wait to be back home. Grey weather and all." The flight had seemed even longer than usual. As if being so close to finally coming home had made those last few hours all the more unbearable. When the plane had made its scheduled stop in Dubai on the way, it had felt like torture having to wait again.

"Not me! I'd sell everything I owned to be going back out there. Sunshine, fabulous beaches and everyone's just so laid back." The woman shrugged her shoulders. "I'll be commuting back to London again by Monday, lucky if I get a seat on the train and then being squeezed on to the tube with barely room to breathe."

"I don't envy you that, I'll admit." Olivia was heading for the Kent coast as soon as she landed and if she thought about it hard enough, she could almost smell the sea air. There was no place in the world she'd rather be.

"So why *are* you so keen to get home?" The woman paused and then held out her hand. "I'm Callie, by the way. Sorry about not introducing myself earlier, but I've been stuck for hours next to people on planes before, who've turned out not to be the sort I'd normally choose to speak to, if you know what I mean?"

"I know exactly what you mean, that's why I plug my headphones in as soon as the plane takes off." She smiled. "I'm Olivia."

"So, tell me Olivia," Callie seemed to hesitate for a moment, giving her an appraising look, "why is it you're so keen to get home. Was your holiday not all you hoped it would be?"

"I haven't been on holiday. I've been living out there for the past few years." Olivia shifted in her seat, realising she'd opened herself up to the inevitable onslaught of questions. So she might as well head them off. "I'm back for my best friend's wedding."

"You're just back home for a holiday, then? No wonder you don't mind the grey skies."

"Actually, I've decided that as I'm coming back anyway, now's as good a time as any to make it permanent." She didn't miss the look of disbelief that crossed Callie's face.

"What can the UK possibly offer you that Oz couldn't?"

"I've just missed friends, family, you know." It wasn't a lie and coming back for Ellie's wedding had reminded her of everything she'd been missing. But it wasn't the whole truth either. Maybe Australia could offer her a lot, but it had also given her things she didn't want anymore. Reminders about mistakes she'd made and years she'd wasted, waiting for someone who'd done nothing but lie to her. If she told Callie the whole story, she'd probably think Olivia was a complete idiot. God knows she'd thought the same herself often enough.

"I suppose." Callie didn't look convinced. "Although, I think I'd still be willing to give it a go."

"Why don't you then?" If her time in Australia had taught Olivia anything, it was that you shouldn't wait around for something to happen; you had to *make* it happen. Sometimes it was just much harder to take your own advice.

"I don't know. Maybe I will."

"Would you go on your own or..." It was strange, asking such a personal question of someone she'd only just met, but it seemed okay somehow.

"Unless I could persuade my sister to give up her boring bank job and come with me." Callie reached into her bag and took out her purse, flapping it open to reveal a photograph. "This is the two of us, when we were little. We're twins and mum used to dress us both the same until we were about twelve and we absolutely refused to put up with it anymore. I couldn't imagine going to Australia without her and I suppose that's what would make me stay here in the end. Even three weeks' back-packing out there without her has been weird."

"It must be nice having that sort of bond." Olivia might not have a sister, but Ellie had been the next best thing. Even better in some ways, with none of the sibling rivalry that sometimes put a strain on family relationships. Ellie was the reason she'd spent so many hours online applying for teaching jobs in Kent, since she'd finally made the decision to leave Australia.

"It is and it's the one reason I'm glad to be home. But you've got your best friend's wedding to look forward to." Callie smiled. "Trouble with getting married here is that you can never guarantee the weather, can you?"

"No, but Ellie's a wedding planner and she runs her own venue. It's beautiful, a gazebo up on the clifftop overlooking the Channel and there's a converted barn too. It should be okay even if the weather lets us down."

"I can see now why you're happy to be home. It certainly beats my commute with strangers lolling on my shoulder or chewing loudly in my ear. And that's before I even get on the tube!" Callie shuddered. "Did you visit home much when you were living in Australia?"

"Not as much as I'd have liked. I suppose I didn't want anyone to see how desperate I was to come home for good and realise I'd failed at this big adventure my life in Australia was supposed to be." It was funny how easy it was to open up to a stranger. She was telling Callie things she hadn't even told Ellie and had barely admitted to herself. But knowing that you were never going to see the person again made it easier to be honest.

"My sister always says you aren't a failure unless you fail to take a chance." Callie laughed. "Maybe I should throw that line back at her when I try to persuade her to come to Australia with me."

"I think you should." The *'fasten seatbelt'* sign illuminated as Olivia spoke and she sat back. When the wheels touched down on the tarmac she'd finally be home for good.

****

"Olivia!" Ellie shouted her name, although she hardly needed to draw attention to herself, given that she was dressed in an oversized hat decorated with corks.

"What on earth are you wearing, El?"

"You're lucky, I very nearly hired a Kangaroo costume to come and pick you up. But even Mum told me I was being silly." Ellie grinned. "I don't care though, I'm just so pleased you're back and I wanted to make you feel at home by bringing a bit of Australia to meet you."

"I am home." Hugging Ellie was even worth getting flicked in the eye with a cork for.

"And you promise you're not going back this time? When you came back for Christmas and then left again, I was sure you were going to change your mind and the lure of..." Ellie hesitated for a minute obviously thinking better of mentioning Josh. "You know what I mean, that the lure of Brisbane's bright lights would leave Channel View Farm completely unable to compete."

"Never. Our holidays with your Aunt Hilary were some of the best days of my childhood." The laughter caught in her throat. "If I'm honest they were probably some of the best days of my life."

"The best is yet to come. I promise." Ellie commandeered the baggage trolley, already heading off in the direction of the exit. "Come on, Mum's baking up a storm for your home coming. So I hope you didn't eat too much on the plane."

"I wasn't hungry and aeroplane food doesn't get any better."

"You know the first thing that my mum's going to say is that you're far too thin, don't you?" Ellie looked over her shoulder, still pushing the trolley at full speed. God help anyone who crossed her path, they'd be bulldozed out of the way.

"Your mum always thinks everyone's too thin, she just wants us to eat more of her cakes." She was virtually having to jog to keep up with Ellie. "Not that I'll need a lot of persuading with her around to cook for me."

"You can eat my share. You do need to put a bit of weight on, now you can put everything that happened out in Australia behind you." Ellie stopped the trolley just for a moment and put an arm around Olivia's waist, giving her a quick squeeze, before taking up the one-woman-trolley-dash again. "Plus, I've got a wedding dress to squeeze into and I think I might have left it a bit late."

"You look great and far less stressed than when I saw you at Christmas." She wished she had half Ellie's energy, although right now the jetlag wasn't helping. "I was expecting you to be hyperventilating into a paper bag by now!"

"It was mum and Alan's wedding that had me like that, as you know!" Ellie finally paused for breath as she pushed the trolley inside the lift up to the car park. "I just wanted it to be perfect for her, even more than I do for the brides who book their weddings with us."

"So, you don't want your own big day to be perfect?"

"It's not that." Ellie pulled a face, looking for a moment just like the six-year-old she'd been when they'd first met. "Sorry, you're probably going to need one of the airline sick bags when I say this, but as long as I'm marrying Ben, it *will* be perfect. The rest is just a bonus."

"You're right I do feel sick!" Olivia laughed as Ellie stuck out her tongue. There was definitely some of that mischievous six-year-old still in there. "I'm only joking, El. I'm really happy for you, honestly I am."

"I know you are and it feels like everything's going right, now you're home." There was that look on Ellie's face again. "Just wait until you see the bridesmaid dress I've got picked out for you."

"Why do I feel nervous?"

"Because you know me too well." Ellie pushed the trolley back out of the lift towards her car, with a determined look on her face, as if Olivia might snatch the trolley off her and head straight back to Brisbane.

"And I'd trust you with my life, but picking out a bridesmaid's outfit when you were tempted to come and pick me up from the airport in a kangaroo costume..."

"Well I can promise that you won't have to dress as an animal."

"Even if you wanted me to wear orange tulle and a Little Bo Peep bonnet, you know I'd be there."

"And I'll do the same for you one of these days."

"I wouldn't hold your breath on that one." Olivia spoke as Ellie pointed her key fob at the car and the boot popped open. Even if she was drawing her pension before Ellie got to be her bridesmaid, it didn't matter. She'd finally accepted she couldn't waste another day waiting for Josh. This was a new chapter of her life and finding love was absolutely the last thing on her mind.

Chapter Two

The thunder started rumbling soon after they left Heathrow and it was almost as though Ellie was trying to outrun it. Despite lightning flashes illuminating the quickly-darkening sky, they still hadn't been caught in any rain when they reached the narrow lanes that led from the main road to Kelsea Bay.

"Ginger will be going mad." Ellie drummed her fingers on the steering wheel as they slowed to a crawl behind a caravan that was too wide to try and pass. "Thankfully Ben has prescribed some medication especially for dogs that struggle when it's stormy, otherwise she pants so much it's like Darth Vader making a dirty phone call."

"Now there's an image I won't be able to get out of my head any time soon! Poor little thing, will the rest of the animals be ok?"

"The donkeys probably wouldn't get spooked unless one of them was actually struck by lightning." Ellie stopped tapping the steering wheel, as the caravan finally turned off into a holiday park only half a mile from Channel View Farm. "But Dolly, the goat, is pregnant, so I can't risk her getting spooked. I usually get her in at night now anyway, just in case."

"I still can't quite believe you're running the farm."

"Me neither. Thankfully I haven't got to try to earn a living from the farming side, otherwise I'd be living on Smart Price noodles and 'surprise' dinners out of dented tins with no labels on." Ellie turned into the farm's driveway. "We've got quite a full diary of wedding bookings for the summer..."

"But?" Ellie had definitely hesitated, but she was already shaking her head.

"But nothing. I was just thinking that I ought to shut the chickens up early too, just in case the storm worries them as well." The corners of Ellie's mouth were twitching. "Have you still got the bird thing, or did spending time in a country where they've got birds bigger than my donkeys finally cure you?"

"I'm getting better, but let's just say I didn't visit any emu farms."

"Maybe we'll leave it until tomorrow to introduce you to the chickens, then." Ellie pulled on the handbrake, as they stopped outside the farmhouse, and opened the car door.

"I'll go and get the goat in, while you sort the chickens out if you like?" As Olivia got out of the car, another flash of lightning briefly lit up the patch of woodland on the far side of the farm.

"Are you sure?"

"Absolutely, if I'm going to be here for the summer, I want to start as I mean to go on."

Taking the lead rope Ellie handed her, Olivia walked down towards the bottom paddock. Thankfully Dolly was easy to catch, mainly because the goat's back was shaped like an aircraft carrier because of the size of her stomach, and for a moment Olivia thought she'd manage to get indoors before the rain came. But all that thunder and lightning hadn't threatened for nothing and, when the rain finally started, it was like being caught inside a car wash. There was so much water it was difficult for her to see where they were going and puddles formed almost immediately on the hard ground, making the goat skip and tug on the lead rope, letting Olivia know she couldn't wait to be inside either.

By the time she put the goat in the stable, her clothes were sticking to her and even her knickers were wet. But there was something about being caught in the rain like that, a feeling of being alive and free she couldn't remember for a long time. Maybe it was being back on the farm evoking so many childhood memories, but whatever it was, it was more than worth wringing out her clothes for. It was priceless.

****

The unmistakable smell of freshly baked cakes greeted Olivia, when she came back downstairs after getting changed.

"I'm so glad you're home!" She was pulled into Ellie's mum's warm embrace before she even had the chance to say hello. Karen had been like a second mother to Olivia in the years since she'd first met Ellie. And, with both of them only children, it was like the extended family they'd never had.

"It smells amazing in here!" Olivia said as Karen finally released her, piles of cakes surrounding them on every work surface.

"Well I've got to admit not all of them are for you." Karen smiled. "But this one is." She gestured towards a plump lemon drizzle cake sitting in pride of place on the middle of the scrubbed pine kitchen table. "It is still your favourite, isn't it?"

"Only when you make it."

"Well I for one am starving." Ellie flicked the kettle on. "And we're both dying to hear what happened when Josh finally realised you were leaving."

"Should I unpack first? My cases are clogging up the hallway..." Olivia couldn't help laughing at the look of horror that crossed Ellie's face.

"I'll help you unpack later." There was no way Ellie was going to let her get away with it, so she might as well get it over with.

"I think he thought I was just bluffing or that I'd got another job nearby. I'd threatened to come back to England so many times that he assumed it was just talk." Olivia took the slice of cake Karen passed to her.

"I've never really got my head around why you didn't come home sooner." Karen's eyebrows knitted together as she spoke. "So, let me get this straight, when you got to Australia, you found out he was already engaged, and then you stayed on for the best part of five years?"

"I know, it sounds crazy. But when we met during that six months' he was on secondment to the school I worked at in London, I thought he was *the one*, if there is such a thing. What we had – or at least what I thought we had - seemed worth the risk of moving to Australia for, when he had to go back. You know how believable he could be from when you met him."

"You don't have to tell me this if you don't want to, but why on earth did you stay on, once you found out he was already engaged?" Karen laid a hand over hers. Olivia had only really told Ellie the whole story, but there was no need to keep up the pretence any more. All hope that things might work out in the end had long since passed.

"He was so good at convincing me that the engagement didn't really mean anything and I really wanted to believe it, so I just kept hanging on." Olivia sighed heavily. "When I found out about Alice, we had a screaming row and I told him we were finished. But I'd committed to a three-year contract and I suppose, at first, I just didn't want to feel like I was letting the children down, or have to come home and admit my big adventure to Australia was actually just a big failure. I didn't want to come back with my tail between my legs and tell everyone that I'd been made a total fool of by the person I thought I'd end up marrying, but who already had a fiancée waiting for him in Brisbane."

"He was a master of mind games though, wasn't he?" Ellie put three cups of tea onto the table in front of them. "Tell mum what he said to you."

"You're going to think I'm really stupid."

"I'd never think anything bad of you." Karen squeezed her hand again. "We've all been fooled by love."

"Thank you." She smiled despite the tears burning at the back of her eyes. The humiliation was worse than anything else now, she was finally starting to get over Josh but coming to terms with wasting years on him was going to be more difficult.

"Like Ellie said, Josh was really good at making me believe it was just a matter of time before we got together. His mum and his fiancée Alice's mum, were really good friends. According to him, they'd more or less arranged the marriage and neither he nor Alice really wanted it. But Josh's mum has a lot of medical issues and they always seemed to be waiting for the next operation or treatment to be out of the way before breaking the news to her that they were ending the engagement."

"And were you still *seeing* Josh the whole time?" Karen gave her an old-fashioned look.

"No. We were working together, but I wouldn't see him outside of work. I told him straight out that we couldn't have a relationship until he was free to completely commit to it." She sighed again. "I never got to meet Alice, to see through the lies he was telling me. It was pretty lonely if I'm honest. I was scared to get close to colleagues in case they found out I'd followed Josh to Brisbane and I couldn't bring myself to date anyone else, because I was still holding out for him to be free. Maybe if I had made friends with some of the other staff at the school, they'd have told me how devoted Alice was to him, but I just wanted to keep myself to myself."

"But what was in it for Josh? That's what I don't understand. You wouldn't see him outside of school, so why didn't he just move on to the next gullible woman he could string along?" Ellie's face dropped as soon as the words were out of her mouth. "God, sorry, Liv. I didn't mean you were gullible..."

"I was. For most of the time anyway." Olivia poked at the delicious slice of lemon cake with her fork, her appetite completely gone. "I think he hoped he'd wear me down and that somehow he'd be able to balance a life with both me and Alice in it. Maybe he was hanging on for that, in the same way I was hoping he might finally be free to be with me properly."

“And then you found out he was getting married?” Karen was frowning again. Staying out there for so long must look insane from the outside.

“Yes, nearly two years ago now. There was an article about it in the Brisbane Times. Alice’s parents are very wealthy apparently and the wedding was huge, with anyone who was anyone in Brisbane invited. Turns out I wasn’t anyone important in Brisbane or in Josh’s life when it came down to it. He didn’t even have the decency to tell me first. One of the other staff pinned the article from the paper up in the staffroom.”

“And you didn’t come home, even then?” Karen was already on her second slice of cake. Was there such a thing as vicarious comfort eating?

“I would have done, but I’d just been promoted to Head of House. I also had a little boy in my class who had selective mutism, he only had about eighteen months left at the school and I was the only member of staff with the specialist training to support him. As a result I stayed on and had to hear all about Josh’s wedding, see the photos that other staff took of the big day. I spent far too long online in the evenings, scrolling through Facebook photos and trying to analyse the look on Josh’s face, wondering if he’d meant anything he said to me and looking for any hint that he didn’t want to marry Alice.”

“Oh Olivia, love.” Karen stood up and wrapped her arms around her again, almost knocking the cake flying in the process. “I’m sorry you went through all of that and so far away from home too.”

“Ellie was great. Even on the other side of the world, she was always there for me.” She looked across and Ellie returned her smile. “The times I could come home, and the visits Ellie and other friends and family made over to Brisbane, were what kept me going. After the wedding, I decided that was it, but I hung on for little Saul. So I suppose Josh never really thought

I'd go. I had to give a term's notice. But even when I handed in a letter of resignation, when I got back from the UK after Christmas, he didn't believe me. He didn't even advertise my post."

"It's because he's a total narcissist." Ellie curled her lip. "He reminds me of Rupert. A lot." Ellie had been engaged before Ben, but to say it hadn't worked out would have been an understatement. And Ellie's dad had deserted her mum when Ellie was still in primary school. So Karen was right, they'd all had their share of heartbreak over the years, which was exactly why Olivia knew they'd understand.

"I did wonder if he ever thought about how I felt." She already knew the answer to that. It had only ever been about Josh. "When he finally realised I was leaving, after I cleared my desk and handed him my keys and security pass, he reacted as if I'd made the decision out of the blue. He even told me I was letting the children down, knowing that would play on my emotions."

"What a nasty piece of work." Karen's cheeks were burning and Olivia had seen that look before, when she'd rushed in to rescue her and Ellie from the local bully when they were kids. "I'd love to give him a piece of my mind. I wasted a lot of years being with Ellie's dad, but I'd do it all again ten times over to have her." Karen looked at her daughter and then back at Olivia again. "I know you can't see it now, but I really believe things happen for a reason and maybe it was what you needed so you don't miss real love when it comes along."

"There speaks a happy, newly-married woman." Olivia couldn't deny the glow Karen had these days. Growing up, she'd seen her work hard as a single mum and Ellie had never missed out on anything as a result. It was so nice that Karen had finally found someone to look after her for once. "Where is the lovely Alan by the way?"

"He's on his way back from a farmer's market in Surrey and he'll be the first one to tell you the same when he gets here. Neither of us ever thought we'd find love and especially not with each other. I couldn't stand him when I first met him!" Karen laughed.

"He was a grumpy old sod and we were worried all we'd inherited from Aunt Hilary, when she left us the farm, was a miserable neighbour!" Ellie grimaced. "But Mum brought out the best in him and now I've got a lovely stepdad."

"I can't believe how much has changed in the last year or so for both of you." Olivia felt that pang again. Ellie and Karen had transformed their whole lives while she'd been in Australia.

"It's been hard work turning an old donkey sanctuary into a wedding venue, but we love it, don't we, Mum?"

"We do. I get to bake all day long and Ellie gets to make brides' dreams come true." Karen wagged a finger at Olivia. "So don't you go worrying about how things are going to turn out for you."

"Well, the first priority is to find a job."

"You can help out here until you do." Ellie had an animated look on her face. "There's always something to do and there's plenty of room in the farmhouse, especially with Mum moving into Alan's place after they got married. In fact, it's been a bit lonely on my own."

"That might be alright until after you and Ben get married, but I promise I'll be gone by then. I can always go up and stay with Mum and Dad in Yorkshire if I need to."

"How are they doing up there?" Karen was clearing the plates away as she spoke and Olivia hoped she wouldn't notice that she'd hardly touched her cake.

"They love it. Moving up that way has meant they could buy a much bigger place and they've been able to offer a home to three foster children now." Olivia was so proud of what her parents were doing with their early retirement, but it made it harder for her to lean on them and even to go and stay. They needed the space and their energy for the children they were looking after, so the last thing she wanted to do was lumber them with an unemployed, thirty-year-old daughter moping around. Even so, she was applying for jobs in Kent and Yorkshire, so she'd just have to let fate decide where she ended up. Wherever the first job offer turned up, was where she'd settle. "They've just had a little boy placed with them and he's having some issues adjusting, so I'm not going to go up and see them just yet, but I will as soon as they think he'll be okay with meeting me."

"It sounds like they're doing an amazing job, but it must be difficult not being able to welcome you home." Karen scraped the cake into a bin marked *'pigs'*, but she didn't make any comment about Olivia not eating it. Knowing Karen, even if she was offended, she'd never say so.

"I think Mum is struggling especially." Olivia shrugged. "But I'm a grown up and I told them I'll be okay."

Karen stopped the scraping and turned to look at Olivia again, as if she was about to say something else, but the sound of tyres crunching against gravel outside the farmhouse stopped her.

"Is that Alan?" Olivia was looking forward to meeting him again and finding out more about the man Karen had married. She'd met him at Christmas, at their wedding, but there'd been too much going on for her to really get to know him.

"I think it might be Ben and Seth, actually." Ellie was peering out of the kitchen window.

"Who's Seth?" Olivia narrowed her eyes. If Ellie and Karen thought that introducing her to one of Ben's friends was a good idea, they were sadly mistaken.

"He's Ben's best man. They met at uni and he's a zoologist, but he's just given up a post at Edinburgh Zoo. So he's taking a couple of months' leave to be around for the wedding and he's staying with Ben at his flat." Ellie was smiling in a way that did nothing to alleviate Olivia's suspicions.

"Please don't tell me you're trying to set me up with him?"

"Me?" Ellie widened her eyes. "Normally I'd say he might be worth going out with, to dip your toes back into the dating game, but he's off to San Diego after the wedding to take up a research post at a zoo over there. Even if he was staying here I'd probably warn you to steer clear, though, because from what Ben says most of his relationships are pretty short-lived. But I'm sure there are some of Ben's other friends in the village we can introduce you to when you're ready."

"Just don't get any ideas, okay?"

"I promise!" Ellie's attempt to look innocent, as Ben and Seth walked into the kitchen, didn't do much to convince her. Seth was taller than Ben, with sandy blond hair and the greenest eyes Olivia had ever seen.

"Lovely to see you again, Liv." Ben kissed her on both cheeks, picking up the shortened version of her name that Ellie so often used. "This is Seth, my best man. And, Seth, this is Olivia, Ellie's bridesmaid and oldest friend."

"Nice to meet you." Seth shook her hand. "Looks like we'll have to get our heads together seeing as these two are determined to have joint hen and stag dos."

"Nauseating, isn't it? Them wanting to do absolutely everything together like that?" She just hoped he'd get the joke and not think she was some bitter Miss Havisham type. God knows how much Ellie had told Ben about what had gone on in Australia and how much he'd told Seth as a result.

"Absolutely toe-curling." Seth winked, a twinkle in those green eyes, and she was sure the run up to the wedding was going to be fun. After all, almost five years of being mostly miserable was more than enough for anyone.

Chapter Three

"What's on the agenda for today then?" Olivia spooned an extra sugar into her coffee, determined to work through the jet lag that was making her eyes feel as though they belonged on a basset hound.

"Well, you should still be in bed for a start." Ellie passed her a plate piled high with toast; she was her mother's daughter and no-one would ever say they went hungry in the Chapman household. When they were children, living in the same street, and Olivia's parents had both worked long hours, she'd loved spending time in Karen's kitchen. It was always warm and there was guaranteed to be something delicious in the oven, or just cooling on the side, and there'd always been enough for Ellie and Olivia to help themselves. It was a good job they'd been constantly on the go, building dens in the little patch of woodland that had given The Copse its name, or racing down the big hill that led to the common, somewhat grandly named *'Silver Jubilee Park'*, but which was really just a rusting swing set and slide that had seen better days. They'd often packed up the box of fairy cakes, or whatever it was that Karen had made for them, and taken Olivia's portable CD player into their latest den. They'd set out a picnic on an old duvet that Olivia's mum had let them take and talk for hours about all the things they were going to do when they grew up. They were going to have a penthouse flat overlooking the Thames and have dinner every night in Pizza Hut. Olivia was going to be a world-famous singer and Ellie was going to write children's books, like Beatrix Potter. It had been an eclectic mix of aspirations, when pizza had seemed the height of sophistication. Ellie had nearly ended up in the penthouse flat too. If she'd stayed with her ex-fiancé, Rupert, a property developer, she could have lived anywhere she wanted, except Rupert had turned out to be every bit as self-centred as Olivia had always suspected. Money came first for him every time and that meant he was nowhere near good enough for her best friend. When he'd asked Ellie to choose between him and the farm, there'd never really been any contest. Ben on the other hand, was perfect for her. Being the local vet, he and Ellie had become close when he'd taken care of the animals her Aunt Hilary had left her, along with the farm. They might never afford a penthouse, but what they had was worth a million times more.

"I think going back to bed would be a mistake, even if my body does feel like lead." Olivia stirred a third spoonful of sugar into her coffee. "Anyway, I want to help out, there must be loads to do keeping this place running."

"Well, I never get bored, put it like that." Ellie smiled. "And if I don't take Gerald's breakfast out to him, be brays loudly enough to wake the dead."

"I forgot to set an alarm this morning, so I was grateful for his wake-up call." Olivia had been in the middle of a dream where she was trying to run away from something, but she couldn't make her legs work, when the sound of the old donkey calling out for his breakfast had woken her up. He'd been a resident on the farm for years, which had been turned into a donkey sanctuary by Ellie's Great Aunt, and Gerald had definitely been the favourite. Growing up, Olivia had spent at least part of every summer holiday at the farm with Ellie and they'd promised they'd carry on every year, even when they were grown up and living in that penthouse flat. Leaving school changed everything, though. Universities in different towns meant their lives moved in different directions, with new groups of friends, followed by very different career paths. They still saw each other, of course, and spoke at least once a week, but their childhood plans were largely forgotten. And then Olivia met Josh and moved to the other side of the world. It was only after the move, she realised how much she still relied on Ellie's unconditional support. She'd been the only person Olivia had felt able to completely confide in and Ellie had never judged her for holding on to the hope that Josh might eventually keep the promises he'd made. As a result, she wanted to do whatever she could to pay Ellie back. "I really want to help out while I'm here, there must be some jobs on the farm you need me to do?"

"I'm sure we can find you something." Ellie didn't even seem to have time to sit down to eat. She was loading up the dishwasher at the same time as eating her toast. Her little dog, Ginger, watching her every move in case a crumb got dropped that she could take advantage of. "But your main priority should be looking for a job around here. I really don't want you to have to move away again, I've missed having you around so much."

"Don't worry, I'm on top of it." Finding the right job was definitely a priority. Despite the issues with Josh in Australia, Olivia had loved the work she'd been doing. Helping children like Saul had made her realise what she really wanted to do. Climbing the ladder to be a head teacher had been her goal when she was newly qualified, but something had shifted over the last couple of years. Making a difference now seemed far more important than having a certain job title.

"Is there anything good going near here?" She didn't miss Ellie's hopeful look. After so long hanging around on the periphery of someone else's life, it was lovely to feel so wanted.

"There's actually a part time job going in Kelsea Bay, but it's only over the summer." Olivia was trying not to get too excited about the possibility of getting work in the town nearest to Channel View Farm. Experience had taught her that when things seemed too good to be true, they usually were.

"It would be great to have you working just down the road, but I don't want it to stop you getting something more permanent. We're really busy here over the summer, with it being wedding season, it's just the winter we're struggling to get bookings for. I could afford to pay you a wage, at least for now. It's why we're not going to have a honeymoon until the autumn, either, we've got to make hay while the sun shines as Aunt Hils used to say."

"I'm definitely up for helping out here, but I wouldn't dream of letting you pay me. Years of hardly having any social life has one upside, I've got quite a lot of money saved up, so it's not that I'm worried about. It's just wanting to feel settled again and getting a full-time job would really help. I've been working my way through a list of the local schools, and writing to them on spec, to see if they might have some vacancies coming up in September. It turns out that one of them is running a camp over the summer for children with special educational needs and the head teacher is recruiting for temporary staff. So, although it's not permanent, I don't think it would hurt to make those sorts of contacts. Teaching jobs in the towns and villages around here are few and far between from what I've seen, so getting to know the head teacher of one of them can't hurt my chances."

"Absolutely and once they see how great you are with the kids, you'll have job offers flooding in." Ellie stopped loading the dishwasher and looked at her. "I'll take you for a tour of the farm, so you can see what's changed since Mum's wedding, but not until you've eaten at least one piece of toast."

"Yes, Mum." Olivia picked up one of the doorstep-thick slices. "You do know that one slice of this is equivalent to about four normal slices of bread, don't you?"

"Trust me, you'll need it. Especially if Alan finds out you're looking for things to do. I think, having been a farmer all his life, he forgets that some of us haven't grown up lugging bales of hay around on our backs, or manually digging drainage ditches. Not that he ever lets Mum overdo it."

"He really adores her, doesn't he?"

"He's besotted." Ellie couldn't keep the smile off her face. "I can't help thinking that Aunt Hilary knew what she was doing when she left us the farm."

"Definitely, and then there's you and Ben. I bet your Aunt Hilary didn't think a lot of Rupert?"

"She couldn't stand him and, as usual, she was right." Ellie finished clearing the last of the plates from the table, giving up on her mission to force feed Olivia toast. "Who knows what a month or two on the farm will bring for you?"

"A new job, hopefully."

"I thought you and Seth hit it off really well last night."

"El, don't. I just want to get my life back on track and, in my experience, relationships just get in the way."

"I'm not! Like I said, Seth wouldn't be right for you anyway but I'm sure there's someone out there who is. Unless you're still in love with Josh?" Ellie frowned, suddenly looking so much like Karen had the night before. That was the thing about best friends, there was no cautiously edging around a sensitive subject.

"No. At least I don't think so." Olivia shrugged. She'd never been able to be anything but honest with Ellie, even when she wanted to hide something. "Part of me hates him, but mostly I just don't feel anything anymore, romantically. For anyone. Maybe I've just shut that part of myself off. A bit like your Aunt Hilary."

"It was different for Aunt Hils." Ellie was still frowning. "She lost the love of her life in the war and there was never anyone who could match up to him. You've had a lucky escape. Don't put your life on hold for him, for any longer than you already have."

"I'm not. I'm looking for a job and I'm more than ready to start a new life, I just don't see that needing to include a man and I certainly won't be basing any of my decisions on that in future. Been there, done that and got a whole wardrobe of tee-shirts."

"Okay, I promise not to interfere in your love life, or the lack of it!" Ellie finally replaced the frown with a smile. "At least not until you're settled around here, with a job. I don't want to drive you away."

"So, have I earned my tour of the farm?" Olivia took a gulp of the sweet black coffee, which was even less appetising now it had gone cold.

"Absolutely, and I've got something I want to show you anyway. If it doesn't restore your faith in love, then nothing will."

"Don't tell me Ben has carved a likeness of your face into the cliff-side?" She laughed as Ellie threw a wet tea towel in her direction.

"Now you're starting to sound like Seth!" Ellie grinned, the sisterly teasing as easy as it always had been. "Come on, let's get outside and you can see what you think."

****

"Well?" Ellie stood to one side of a series of arches, leading towards the wedding gazebo.

"It's beautiful." The wooden arches were inlaid with delicate lattice work, which looked like lace and matched the sides of the gazebo. "Who built it?"

"Alan." Ellie was as proud as if she'd done the work herself. "He said he wanted to honour Aunt Hilary and thank her for bringing Mum into his life. After he built the arches, he spent ages with Mum transplanting mature climbing roses, so it would look as good as possible straight away. Eventually the roses should grow right up over the arches, but I think it looks pretty spectacular already, don't you?"

"Hilary would have loved it." Olivia felt a lump in her throat. It must be amazing to have someone create something so beautiful, as a thank you for coming into their life. Ellie was right, it couldn't fail to restore your faith in love, at least for other people. "I bet you've got three padlocks on Gerald's gate now!"

"More like four!" Ellie laughed. The old donkey was infamous for his ability to escape from his paddock and he'd nearly ruined the farm's first ever wedding, when he and Dolly the goat had got out of their field and eaten all the flowers and most of the wedding cake. "Is that your phone?"

"I hadn't even realised it was ringing." Olivia looked at the screen, it was a number she didn't recognise. "Sorry, I should get this, in case it's about a job."

"Of course. Do you want me to leave you to it?" As Ellie spoke, Olivia shook her head. She had no secrets any more.

"Hello. Olivia Gates speaking."

"Oh, brilliant, I was expecting to leave a voice mail." The relief in the man's voice was tangible. "It's Peter Coleman, you sent in an application for the summer camp teaching job at St Thomas College?"

"That's right." She held her breath. The logical part of her brain telling her that people didn't usually ring up to say your application had been unsuccessful. In fact, you were lucky to hear anything at all, unless they wanted to interview you.

"I was looking to appoint one part-time teacher, but now one of the other teachers has pulled out because of a family emergency and frankly I'm desperate."

"I'll try not to take that as an insult." Olivia couldn't help laughing. It might not have been flattering, but if it meant she was guaranteed a job, a few minutes from the farm, she could live with it.

"Sorry, sorry, I didn't mean it like that." Peter Coleman sounded distinctly flustered and Olivia liked him already. "What I meant was, that looking at your CV, if your references check out, I think the interview will just be a formality. You've got a lot more experience than I ever dreamt I'd get from a temporary teacher. Is there any way you could commit to more than two days a week, if you want the job, that is?"

"I could probably do three days a week, if things feel right when we meet in person." She'd taken a leap of faith once before and that hadn't exactly worked out, so she was learning to be more cautious.

"You can't go full-time then, to cover both posts?" There was a slightly pleading tone to Peter's voice.

"I'm really sorry, but I've already agreed to help my friend out with her business a couple of days a week." Olivia looked over at Ellie who was shaking her head, she wouldn't hold Olivia to her promise but it was one she was determined to keep. Spending time with her best friend was even more of a priority than finding a job in the short term.

"Well, let's say three days then and I'll work something out for the other two. Can you meet me at the school this afternoon, so we can just formalise everything? You said in your email that you've got your police check paper work all up to date?"

"Yes, I can bring that all over with me. How about three o'clock, would that suit you?"

"Perfect, I look forward to meeting you then."

"Thank you." Olivia ended the call and was nearly knocked flying by Ellie running towards her.

"Have you got an interview?"

"I think it's a bit more than that. If we get on okay when we meet later, he wants to give me the job. He's just got to check my references out."

"Will he have to ring, Josh?" Ellie took a step back and grimaced. Josh wouldn't last five minutes if he ever crossed Ellie's path and the thought made Olivia smile again.

"No, the head teacher from the school in Brisbane does all the references for teaching staff and she told me I was welcome back anytime. I think she had an idea that something went on between me and Josh when he was in the UK, but she only ever judged me on my work."

"Is it the job in Kelsea Bay, with the summer camp?"

"Yes." It was the news Olivia had been hoping for, a reason to stay in Kent.

"I think news this good calls for a celebratory dance!" Ellie suddenly started to hum and put one hand in front of her, with the palm upturned, and then the other.

"The Macarena? Really!" Olivia laughed. When they'd been at primary school they'd spent hours perfecting their moves and Ellie hadn't forgotten any of them. It had been their slightly embarrassing *'go to'* dance ever since. They'd done it at Olivia's leaving party when she'd been heading off for a new life in Australia. And even, by special request of the bride, at Karen and Alan's wedding.

"Come on, don't leave me hanging!" By now she had her hands on her hips and was jumping backwards.

"I can't believe you're making me do this." Despite her protests, Olivia fell in step beside her friend and the years were peeled back in an instant. It was going to be all right, it really was. She was dancing on a cliff top above the English Channel and she almost certainly had a new job, working with children who needed her even more than she needed them. She had a weird feeling, something she couldn't identify at first, and then she finally realised what it was. She was happy, for the first time in a very long while.

Chapter Four

"Have you delivered art therapy before?" Peter Coleman looked at Olivia over his half-moon spectacles, his flowery shirt straining across his stomach, which bounced up and down when he laughed. Give him a long white beard and he'd make a very good Father Christmas, if he ever decided to retire as head teacher of St Thomas College, a private primary school on the edge of Kelsea Bay.

"I did a lot of art therapy, music and drama projects with the children I taught in Australia. It really seemed to bring out their creative side, even for the students with the most severe special needs." She smiled as Peter nodded his head and put another tick on the clipboard he was holding. It was the most informal interview she'd ever had. They were walking and talking as he showed her around the school, which would be hosting the summer camp, whilst its regular pupils were on their eight-week summer break. Peter had explained that the school ran as a charity, with the fees from private pupils funding places for children from disadvantaged backgrounds, as well as the summer camp and a school in Africa for children who wouldn't receive an education otherwise. It made her decision, to work in the private sector for a while, feel a lot less like she was selling out.

"Your paperwork from the school in Brisbane all checked out by the way." Peter was already heading out of the door of the well-stocked art studio. It certainly didn't look like they'd be short of materials at the summer camp. "Your head teacher there couldn't say enough good things about you in her email. It sounds like they were very sorry to lose you. Weren't you tempted to stay out there?"

"I've been asked that a few times since I got back, but I can't say I was. It just felt like the right time to come home."

"And is this home, then? Tucked down here in Kelsea Bay?"

"It is for me. Probably not as ambitious as I'm supposed to be, but spending all that time in Brisbane made me realise what it is I really want and where I want to be."

"So, will you be looking for a permanent job around here in September?" Peter narrowed his eyes, as if he still wasn't quite convinced it was what Olivia really wanted.

"That's the plan." Olivia sighed. "But I think I missed the boat, most of the vacancies for September have already been advertised. Although I can always pick up some supply teaching if I need to."

"Well, there's a possibility there might be something going here. If things work out over the summer and you'd be interested in applying?" Peter had a way of pausing at the end of a sentence that made Olivia desperate to fill the silence with an answer. It must have been really useful when he was trying to find out if any of his pupils were up to no good.

"Of course I'd be interested!" Olivia failed spectacularly at playing it cool. "I did have a look on your website, but there was nothing on there."

"It's been one of those weeks!" Peter had picked up the pace now, as he led Olivia away from the main school building, along the side of a car park. He had quite a turn of speed for such a large man. "Lucinda, the member of staff who had to pull out of the summer camp, received some unexpected news about her husband's job. It looks like they might have to relocate to Canada by the end of the summer and so that means I'll be looking to replace the farm manager. They've gone out there now to finalise the details and try to find somewhere to live."

"Oh." Olivia felt her enthusiasm draining away. "I'm really sorry but I don't think I'd be any use to you. The only experience I've got is helping my friend and her place isn't even a working farm anymore."

"Sorry, sorry, I'm talking in riddles again! Like I say, it's been one of those weeks. First that vacancy came up unexpectedly and then I got the go ahead from the school trustees to put in a funding application for a new post. Which means that as well as having to think about advertising the farm manager's job, after I thought all the vacancies for next term were filled, I've had to put together a proposal for a special needs teaching position to support some of the children who'll be starting with us in September. I should hear back from them any time about whether we can go ahead."

"I'd love to be considered if the post gets approved." This interview was turning into a rollercoaster ride.

"Absolutely." Peter waved his arms, as if there'd never been any question. "This is the farm and the manager leads sessions here with all of the pupils for at least one lesson a week. There's about ten acres altogether and the children at the summer camp will be able to make use of it too. If I can find someone to replace Lucinda that is."

"Wow, the facilities you have here are amazing. Is that a sand school over there?" Olivia pointed to a fenced area to the right of the paddock they were standing next to. It brought back memories of the riding lessons she'd had as a kid, before her instructor had told her in no uncertain terms that she just didn't have the aptitude for riding and that her parents should stop wasting money on something she'd never get the hang of. She'd tried gymnastics after that and then dance classes, but she'd never really found a hobby she'd been any good at. So, it made her more determined than ever to help the children she taught to realise their full potential, especially when some other people had written them off.

"Yes. We were hoping to work with the local Riding for the Disabled group at the summer camp. They were going to lend us a couple of their ponies, as Lucinda used to volunteer with them and she's qualified to instruct." Peter paused. "I don't suppose you're qualified to teach riding too?"

"As much as I'd like to help, I barely know one end of the horse from the other." Olivia echoed her old riding instructor's words; still remembering how it felt to be told you were useless at something you enjoyed. "I hope it's not going to be a deal breaker though?"

"Absolutely not, you seem to have Hugo's seal of approval already and he knows everything that goes on at the farm." Peter bent down to stroke the head of a black and white cat that had wandered over and sat on one of Olivia's feet. "It looks like he doesn't want you to leave."

"I can't tell you how happy I am to be able to work here over the summer."

"The feeling is entirely mutual." Peter straightened up and stuck out his hand. "Shall we shake on it and officially welcome you to the St Thomas College summer camp?"

"Thank you." Olivia took his hand and barely resisted the urge to hug him. He didn't just look like Father Christmas, he'd given her as welcome a gift as anything St Nick had ever delivered.

****

Despite Ellie's offer to lend her car, Olivia had decided to walk down to Kelsea Bay for her interview and she was glad she had, even though the walk back up to Channel View Farm – perched as it was on the clifftops – was pretty steep. It was almost five o'clock by the time the interview finished, but the sun was still as warm as it had been at lunch time and the July weather had lived up to its promise for once. It was winter back in Brisbane. The idea popped into her head and she immediately blocked it out, not wanting to take up a second longer thinking about the life she'd left behind.

She wasn't concentrating when the car came past her and she barely noticed it until she heard the squeal of brakes and someone shouting.

"Casper!" The car had stopped about thirty feet in front of her and a woman, still wearing her slippers, had come out of a driveway and was peering under the front of the car.

Please don't let it be a child. Olivia's legs didn't seem to be moving and it felt forever before she got level with the car. An elderly man was sitting in the driver's seat, his knuckles white as they gripped the steering wheel.

"He's hit the dog!" The woman was cradling a small curly-coated black dog, which was whining. Although it didn't look to Olivia like it had sustained any serious injury.

"Shall I call the vet?" It was funny, she'd have known exactly what to do if it had been a person who'd been injured. But was there such a thing as an animal ambulance? At least she could phone Ellie and ask her to get hold of Ben.

"Thank you." The woman managed a wobbly smile. "Is Bert alright?"

"Bert?" She'd been sure the woman had called the dog Casper.

"My husband, he was the one driving."

"He's your husband?" Olivia pulled up the handle and opened the door of the car slowly, not wanting to frighten the man who still hadn't even turned to his head. "Are you okay, Bert?"

"I didn't see him, I'd almost stopped to back into the drive and he just shot out in front of me. Is he... is he *dead*?" Bert's voice cracked on the word and Olivia placed her hand gently on his shoulder.

"No, he doesn't look badly hurt from what I can see. Your wife's looking after him."

"Hetty will kill me if anything happens to Casper and I couldn't live with myself either." Bert was still gripping the steering wheel and Olivia wondered if she was going to have to prise his hands off to get him to move.

"I'm sure it wasn't your fault. I'm just going to phone the vet and then we can get you indoors, I think you could use a nice cup of tea to settle your nerves." She was definitely home. What could be more British than solving a problem with tea?

Just as Olivia got her phone out of her pocket, another car pulled up in front of Bert's and, for once, luck seemed to be on her side, as Ben and Seth got out of the car.

"Has the dog been hit?" Ben moved to crouch next to the woman who was still holding the dog in her arms, although it seemed to be struggling to get free. The shock Bert had suffered meant he'd almost certainly come off worse.

"I thought I'd shut the front door after the man from the catalogue delivered my new duvet covers, but I can't have done it properly. And when Casper heard Bert's car pulling up, he ran out before I could stop him."

"Don't worry, we'll get him sorted out. I think you've brought Casper into the veterinary surgery to see me before. It's Mrs Sanders, isn't it?" Ben had the sort of soothing tone that a lot of doctors could learn something from.

"Yes, that's right, but he's never had anything seriously wrong with him before."

"He doesn't look hurt, but we can get him into my car and take him down to the surgery to take a better look and see if we need to get any x-rays done." Ben looked up at Olivia and smiled, as Seth handed him a blanket he'd taken out of the boot of the car.

"Is everyone else okay?" Seth looked straight at her. "You weren't caught up in the accident were you, Olivia?"

"No, I was just walking home, but I think Bert's a bit shaken up."

"Are you okay?" Seth leant into the open car door and Bert finally turned his head.

"My legs feel like jelly."

"It's just a bit of shock, but the dog's going to be fine, so perhaps Olivia can take you inside?"

"I'm not sure my legs will hold me up. I really thought I'd killed him when I heard that bump." Bert's hands were shaking when he finally took them off the steering wheel.

"Do you need me, Ben? Or can I stay here with Olivia and get Bert settled indoors?" Seth turned to his friend and Ben nodded in response.

"That's fine. If Mrs Sanders is okay to come along with me, I can drop her home again once we're sure there's definitely nothing to worry about with Casper."

"Thank you." Mrs Sanders allowed Ben to lift the dog gently off her lap and Seth helped her to her feet. "I couldn't bear to leave Casper on his own, but if you don't mind keeping an eye on Bert until we're sure everything's okay, that would put my mind at rest."

"Of course, it's not a problem at all." Olivia supressed a smile. Bert obviously knew he came second place to the dog that was now licking Ben's face. She realised it was going to be up to her and Seth to give him the TLC he needed.

Within a couple of minutes, Ben and Hetty Sanders, still wearing her slippers, had set off for the surgery. Seth was steadying Bert, who despite several reassurances that Casper was almost certainly none the worse for wear, was still unsteady on his feet.

"Shall I put the kettle on?" Olivia turned to Bert, wondering if he really wanted two strangers in his house, but he was nodding his head.

"Oh yes, a tea with two sugars would work wonders and I think I could use a biscuit too, that flipping dog has taken five years off my life. There should be some biscuits in the tin by the kettle, but, if not, I'll let you into a secret, there's some chocolate digestives hidden on the top shelf of the larder that

Hetty can't reach." He laughed, looking much better than he had a few minutes before. "After all, a man's got to have some secrets, hasn't he? Even after fifty-two years of marriage."

"That's a real achievement." Seth smiled as Bert finally let go of his arm and led them into a sunny kitchen, which looked as though it hadn't changed much since he and Hetty had first got married. It was so retro that it was almost fashionable again and Olivia immediately felt at home.

"Can I get you a drink, Seth?" She didn't miss how he pulled out a chair for Bert and waited for the older man to get comfortable. She'd almost forgotten there were still some genuinely nice guys about.

"I'd love a tea, no sugar for me though, thanks." Seth picked up the biscuit tin and put it in front of Bert.

"Sit down, lad. It's like having Hetty standing over me otherwise, making sure I don't eat too many of these." He took the lid off and stacked four biscuits in front of him before passing the tin to Seth. "Although I know she's only doing it to look after my health. The old girl might not give you the impression she wants to keep me around, but I know she does really."

Olivia turned her back on Seth and Bert to pour the tea. Would Josh and Alice last fifty-two years? Somehow, she doubted it and she wished she could stop thinking about him all together. Wondering what he was doing and if he ever gave her a second thought. But she'd spent so long thinking about Josh, imagining what he was up to and who he was with, it was hard to just switch that off. She had to retrain herself to think about something else, so she pictured Ellie and Ben. There was a couple who could be together as long as Bert and Hetty.

"Here you go." She set the cups out on the table and took a seat next to Bert.

"So how long have you two been courting?" He looked from Seth to Olivia, as he dunked the first chocolate biscuit in his tea.

"We're not a couple. We're just friends." Olivia sipped her tea, even though it was far too hot. She didn't even know why Bert's words had made her feel uncomfortable, but they had.

"Shame. You'd make a handsome couple. Just like me and Hetty in our day."

"Have you always lived in Kelsea Bay?" Seth was clearly keen to change the subject.

"Yes, man and boy. We bought this house a couple of years after we got married. We lived with Hetty's parents for the first two years while we saved hard. We brought all three of our kids up here, but now that they're gone, it's Casper who rules the roost."

"We're both visitors to the area." Seth smiled briefly in Olivia's direction. "We could do with your expertise. We're looking for some ideas for things to do locally for a joint hen and stag day for our friends."

"Never had those sort of shenanigans in my day." Bert smiled despite his words. "A couple of drinks down the pub with my mates to steady my nerves was all I did before me and Hetty got hitched."

"Sounds like you had the right idea." Ellie wouldn't want a lot of fuss and she certainly wasn't the sort of person who'd want to parade around town in a sash with 'L' plates pinned to her back. Olivia just hoped Seth wasn't going to come up with anything Ellie would hate.

"Well we definitely don't want to do the usual night clubs or pub crawls, I think something outside would work best. They're both animal mad and it's what brought them together. So, if we could theme it to that, I reckon we'd be on to a winner.' Seth looked in her direction and she nodded. It sounded much better than just spending the night in a crowded pub. And if hadn't been for Ellie inheriting an ancient donkey along with the farm, she wouldn't have got to know the local vet at all.

"But we need to make sure it isn't a busman's holiday for them. It needs to be something they wouldn't do every day." She could always ask Karen if she could think of something; Ellie's mum had a much better idea what was going on locally than Olivia did.

"My grandson runs boat trips out of the harbour to go seal watching." Bert looked from Seth to Olivia. "Although it's not as relaxing as it sounds, it's in one of those big rubber dinghy things and they go pretty fast. When the boat flies up after it hits a wave, your stomach goes up with it."

"It sounds like it could be perfect." Olivia turned to Seth, who was already nodding. It was something Ellie and Ben would enjoy doing, but with just enough action to please the more adventurous of their friends.

"I'll get you his card, I think it's pinned to the noticeboard over there. I suppose I should warn you that Hetty felt seasick for a week after she went on it and she didn't nag me for days about doing any chores." Bert laughed. "I keep asking her when we can book up to go again! Although, all that said, I do miss her telling me what to do when she'd not around for a bit. I should have listened when she asked me to put a new latch on the gate and then Casper wouldn't have been able to run straight out of the front door into the road. It's just that the battery won't charge on my electric screwdriver anymore and I just can't hold my old manual one tightly enough, since the arthritis has made it so hard to grip properly."

"I think the least we can do is to sort out your gate before we leave. Seeing as you've solved our party dilemma." Seth took the business card that Bert handed him, just as Olivia's phone pinged announcing the arrival of a text.

🖂 Incoming text from Ellie

Hi Liv. Ben just rang as he hasn't got your number and Seth left his phone in the car. Casper is fine, so please tell Mr Sanders not to worry. Ben will drop Casper and Mrs Sanders off in about twenty minutes. How did the interview go? Scratch that, you can tell me when you get home xx

✉ Outgoing text from Olivia
Thanks! That's such a relief. Interview great, but will tell all over a glass of something celebratory later xx

"That was Ellie. Casper's absolutely fine and Ben's bringing him and your wife back home soon." Olivia smiled as the elderly gentlemen who couldn't hold a screwdriver the way he used to, punched the air at the news. It clearly wasn't just Hetty who loved that dog.

"I can't thank you enough. You've all been so brilliant and this young man fixing the gate might just keep me out of the dog house, if you'll pardon the pun!"

****

It only took Seth a few minutes to sort out the gate but, when they waved Bert goodbye, anyone would have thought they'd given up a week's holiday just to help him out.

"He's a real character." Seth turned to her as they walked up the lane from Bert's house. Having decided against waiting for Ben, Seth was keeping her company on the walk back to Channel View Farm. She only hoped she'd still be able to talk and breathe as the climb got steeper.

"I suspect Hetty is even more of a character." Olivia smiled. "Although I got the impression he actually likes being bossed around!"

"My grandparents were like that, they bickered all the time and sometimes I wondered if they actually liked each other, but when my nan died, my granddad was lost without her. We think he died of a broken heart, even though the doctors told us there was no such thing."

"I'm sorry."

"Thanks, but it was a few years back now. I lived with my grandparents most of the time when I was growing up, though, because both of my parents are in the army and they were away a lot, so I was really close to them. Bert reminded me of my granddad so much and I guess it's what we all want, isn't it? The sort of relationship where even the arguments can't change the bottom line, when you love someone, you love them. Even if they drive you mad half the time!"

"I think that's real life, isn't it?" Olivia was struggling to keep up with Seth's long stride, at this rate she was going to have to ask if they could stop for a sit down.

"It is, but romantic movies have a lot to answer for. Us blokes just can't live up to the promise most of the time." Seth raised an eyebrow.

"So is that why you're single?"

"That's straight to the point!" He laughed. "I don't know, really. I've moved around quite a lot with my job and I've just never felt that connection with someone that Ben has with Ellie - when you've got so much in common that you know it's just meant to be. I'm in danger of sounding like one of those movie scripts myself now, aren't I?"

"No, I think you're right. When I look at Ellie and Ben, I just know it's going to work out for them. It's a shame I can't trust my own judgement when it comes to relationships."

"Ben mentioned you'd had a bit of a rough time." Seth didn't push her for details, but that made her want to tell him. She paused by a rusty metal five bar gate, that looked like it could do serious damage if someone or something brushed up against it; but the herd of Friesian cows grazing in the field beyond didn't look as though they had any plans to try and escape.

"I've basically been single since I left the UK to move to Australia." Olivia couldn't look Seth in the eye as she recounted the story, so she watched the cows lazily flicking away flies with their tails, not a worry in the world other than how much grass they could get through. "I met Josh when he was working in London and we clicked in exactly the way you describe. We both loved our work as primary school teachers and the school in Australia, he was taking a sabbatical from, had a big special needs department. He told me he didn't want our relationship to be just a holiday romance and there was a job going at his school, if I was willing to take the chance and see if we could make a proper go of things and start a life together in Australia."

"I take it things didn't go to plan?"

"Ben hasn't told you?" Seth shook his head and she liked Ben even more. If Ellie could trust him with her best friend's secrets, she'd be able to trust him with a whole lot more. "I think it's probably an understatement to say things didn't go to plan. He was already engaged to someone else, who he'd forgotten to even mention when we dated in London."

"That must have been terrible."

"I think he was delusional, as if he actually thought he could make a double life work. But as soon as I found out about Alice, I stopped seeing him. I wouldn't do that to her and I wasn't going to be anyone's second choice... Except that I kept waiting and hoping he might make me his first choice after all. How sad is that?"

"It's not sad. You'd given up a lot to be with him and you can't just turn off your feelings overnight."

"True, but it took me years!" Heat swept across her cheeks and she concentrated even harder on looking at the cows so that she wouldn't have to read the expression on Seth's face.

"Hey, none of this is on you." He put a hand on her arm. "Normal people don't go around lying to other people and playing with their lives, like Josh did to you. This is all down to him and there's absolutely nothing wrong with what you did. A lot of people would have made sure his fiancée found out, for a start. You've got nothing to reproach yourself for."

"Maybe..." Either way, that was enough talk about Josh for one day. "Shall we head up to the farm? I've got my breath back now, so I can stop pretending to find the patterns on those Friesian cows fascinating!"

"Have you got enough breath to tell me about the job interview?"

"It was brilliant." She felt her heart lift just thinking about it. This was going to be the start of something good. Despite not entirely trusting her judgement anymore, she was sure of it.

"When do you start?"

"Next week, but I'm only going to do three days because I want to be around to help Ellie out and then there's everything we need to get sorted for the wedding!"

"So you weren't after a full-time job then?"

"No, but the head teacher tried to persuade me to take one. They've just had a member of staff pull out." The back of Olivia's neck prickled. Had she been selfish to tell Peter she couldn't help out more? She shook her head, she didn't have the skills Peter was looking for anyway. "The trouble is they need someone who has experience of farm work and teaching riding to children with disabilities. So I couldn't really have helped out, even if I hadn't already promised Ellie."

"Do you think they might want me to help out? I've been volunteering with Riding for the Disabled for nearly fourteen years now and I did my instructor's qualification not long after I started out."

"I had no idea." She felt stupid for saying it. Why would she? They'd only just met. There were probably a million and one things she'd never know about Ben's best friend.

"When I was in the sixth form at school I told them that I wanted to be a zoologist, but the closest work experience they could get me was at the local stables!" He laughed. "At first, I had the right hump about it, like a typical teenager, but I soon found out I loved it. I haven't always been able to help very often, especially in recent years, but I can honestly say it's one of the most rewarding things I've done. I'd be happy to volunteer and give them a hand if they're really stuck. If it's not stepping on your toes, that is?"

"Not at all! It would be such a shame if the kids had to miss out." She didn't add that it would be nice to have a friendly face around. Having deliberately kept her distance from her colleagues in Australia, she was nervous about starting somewhere new. What if she'd forgotten how to make friends? "I'll give the head teacher a call when we get home and I'm sure he'll want to take you up on the offer." As they rounded the next corner, the farmhouse came into view. The running repairs might make it a money pit, but it never failed to take her breath away as the land behind it disappeared from view, where the sea seemed to come up and meet it. She'd only been back a couple of days and she'd already landed a new job and found a new friend in Seth. Summer at Channel View Farm was shaping up to be just what she needed.

****

"So, what do you think of Olivia then?" Ben shot Seth a look, as he got them both a drink. "The two of you looked like you were in deep conversation when I passed you on my way back to the farm after I dropped off Hetty Sanders and her dog."

"She's great and if I hadn't already been warned off, I'd probably ask her if she fancied going for a drink." Seth watched his friend's face, but he didn't need to read his expression because he was already vigorously shaking his head.

"You know as a rule I wouldn't even attempt to stand in your way, but if anything happens to make Liv regret coming to stay at the farm, Ellie will kill us both."

"I don't blame Ellie for protecting her." He sat in the armchair opposite Ben's position on the sofa, glad they could slip back into their old habits without any awkward readjustment. They'd shared a flat for more than two years, when they'd been at university, but that hadn't been a guarantee that they would still get on as well as they always had.

People changed over the years and he'd wondered if Ben might have become more like his sister once he owned his own place – shoving a coaster under your drink even on the hideous 1970s Formica table they'd picked up from a boot fair in their first term of living together. Ben's sister, Daisy, had only been a visitor, although a bit too frequent a visitor for Seth's liking. But she'd insisted on buying some coasters and then huffing loudly when she realised that the only time they ever got used was when she was there to make sure that boys definitely couldn't be boys.

Not that he and Ben had been total slobs, but they'd been laid back, both of them more interested in chasing a rugby ball around a muddy pitch, when they weren't studying, than they were in keeping house. Ben's flat was tidy and they'd both grown up a lot, but he still didn't hyperventilate if Seth put a cup down without a coaster. Otherwise staying with him could have been a very long two months.

"She's been through a lot, that's all." Ben took a sip of his beer and shook his head again. "It's a shame you're going away, otherwise the two of you could have been perfect for each other. Even Ellie says that. She'd have let you take the risk, if things were different."

"Listen to you, you sound like an old married man already, waiting for your wife to give you permission!" Seth laughed. Ben knew he was only joking, he'd liked Ellie from the moment he met her and she wasn't the sort to lay down the law with anyone. Except when it came to Olivia. "She told me a bit more about what happened on the way back from the Sanders place. Josh sounds like the sort of man who gives us all a bad name."

"He does, but let's face it, you haven't got an entirely spotless record when it comes to relationships, have you?"

"That's a bit harsh!" Seth laughed again. Ben was giving as good as he got. "I've never lied to any of the women I've dated. It's just that there's always seemed to be a natural end point for me and they just haven't always been on the same wavelength."

"Maybe because your natural end point always comes when things start looking serious." Ben lifted up his bottle of beer. "One of these days you're going to have to take a chance on someone and see if you can make a proper go of things. I don't want you to end up one of those people who's found seeping through the floorboards six months after they've died."

"I'm hoping I can rely on you to come and give me a game of dominos or something, when we're in our nineties. Anyway, I'm sure you and Ellie will have children, so I can always be a doting godfather to them and guilt trip them into visiting me once in a while!"

"It could be worse, anyway, you could be Nathan. I don't think my brother-in-law even breathes in and out without Daisy's permission since she found out she was having a baby." Ben signed. "There's not many people who could put up with Daisy. Not that she appreciates it, for some reason she still holds a candle for you despite the fact she's married to someone else."

"She'd have ended up hating me if we'd ever gone out together. I think she only really liked me because I turned her down."

"I'm almost certain you're right. I love my sister, but she doesn't do well with not getting what she wants."

"It's only me!" Daisy swung open the door of the flat. Almost as if she'd been listening outside and just waiting until her name was mentioned. But judging by the look on her face she hadn't overheard anything, otherwise she definitely wouldn't have been smiling.

"I've know you've got a key Daze, but you could still knock before you charge in like that." Ben stood up and kissed his sister on the cheek. "We could have been sitting here in our underpants for all you knew."

"Is that what you usually do in the evening?" She wrinkled her nose and plumped up the cushion at the other end of the sofa before sitting down, without waiting to be invited.

"Well, no, but you never know."

"It's a risk I'm willing to take Benji." Daisy waved her hand to dismiss her brother's protests, which didn't surprise Seth one bit. She'd never realise her brother just wanted a bit of personal space and privacy and that, just because she had a key to the flat, it didn't mean she had to use it *every time* she came round. Explaining something to Daisy that she didn't want to hear was like shouting into the wind. "So what were you two talking about?"

Seth had been about to say 'you', but that would have been a big mistake. Daisy would want to know exactly what had been said and that definitely wasn't a good idea. "We were talking about Olivia, actually."

"Apparently she's lovely, although I haven't had the chance to meet her yet." Daisy didn't look convinced. "But she's not right for you, though."

"Really? Why's that?" Against his better judgement Seth had to ask, although he somehow doubted that Daisy's opinion was based on anything other than her conviction that she was always right.

"She's far too nice for you from what Ellie's said. You need someone to keep you on your toes."

"Is that so?"

"Umm, just a shame you boys can't always recognise who, or what, is right for you when it comes along." Daisy pulled a face and Seth forced a smile. It wasn't a conversation he wanted to get into and he felt sorry for Nathan. Sometimes it was better to say nothing at all.

"So, to what do we owe the pleasure of this visit?" Ben sat back down at the opposite end of the sofa to his sister. "Do you want a coffee or anything?"

"No! Too much caffeine is bad for the baby. Have you got any coconut water?"

"I've got tap water or some sparking mineral water, that's about it I'm afraid." Ben stood up again and Seth wouldn't have been surprised if he'd offered to try and get some coconut water from one of the local shops. Although he couldn't imagine anywhere in Kelsea Bay stocking it, except perhaps the deli that Daisy ran herself.

"Not tap water, that's full of horrid stuff too. I suppose the mineral water is *fine*." The expression on Daisy's face wasn't convincing. She had a real knack of making people feel guilty for not being able to meet her needs. Seth had seen so much of it over the years. Deep down she was good-hearted and she obviously loved her little brother, but the whole family seemed to have got used to pandering to her.

"How's Nathan?" Seth turned to look at Daisy as Ben got her drink. She looked really well, so all the research she must have done about what was best for her and the baby was clearly paying off.

"He's fine. That's why I'm here actually. He's nagging me to slow down a bit and we're also thinking about what we'll do when the baby's here, in terms of getting a nanny in place."

"Are you wanting one of us to take some of your shifts at the deli?" Seth laughed, although he wouldn't have put it past her.

"Don't be silly." She shot him a look that left him in no doubt what she thought of his joke. "In fact, I need to talk to Ben and I'm not sure it's a good idea that you're here when I do."

"I've got no secrets from Seth. So unless it's something you want to keep secret, then I'm not going to send him to sit in his bedroom." Ben put the water in front of his sister and sat back down next to her on the sofa. For once he wasn't letting Daisy get her own way and Seth was grateful to him. Not that he'd have had any problem going to his room or out for a walk, if Ben had wanted him to, but it was another reminder of why he and Ben had stayed so close even after their work had kept them apart for long periods since they'd left university. It had always felt like he had Ben's unquestioned backing in life. It was almost harder having this time together again, living in the same place and realising just how important old friendships were, when he was about to head to America.

"Well it's nothing *secret*. It's just about the money I invested in the surgery."

"Right." Ben's voice was quiet and Seth suddenly wished he had gone for a walk. Ben had told him when he'd first bought into the surgery that Daisy had invested with him. They'd both been left money by their grandmother and, in one of her grand gestures, Daisy had offered to lend Ben her share too. As a result, he'd not only been able to become a partner in the practice, he'd also bought the flat solely in his name. She was like that, every so often she'd surprise you and be so generous and thoughtful that you could almost forget how difficult and demanding she was a lot of the time.

Seth was also aware that Ben had been saving hard to invest some money into Channel View Farm. Ellie and her mum had apparently put every penny they had into renovating the farm and setting up the business; but they only had summer bookings and they'd been thinking about applying for planning permission to set up an indoor soft play centre to give them some guaranteed income over the winter. Ben had told Seth how much it would cost to set up and, although they could get a mortgage on the farm, Ellie didn't want it to be so big that her mum might end up risking her investment too. The farm had so much potential, but the upkeep of an old house and the conversion of outbuildings didn't come cheap. So if Daisy was about to ask for her money back it would scupper all the plans they had, unless they wanted to mortgage the farm up to the maximum and, according to Ben, Ellie was already having sleepless nights.

"I know it's probably not the best time for you, with the wedding and all." Daisy swirled the mineral water around in her glass. If she thought the wedding was the main issue, she clearly didn't have any idea about Ben and Ellie's plans for the farm. "But with the baby and having to get a temporary manager in at the deli, and thinking about a nanny for afterwards - when I want to go back at least part-time - we really need the money as a bit of a cushion. And, of course, there are things I want to do to the nursery, plus the Silver Cross pram I've got my eye on is three thousand pounds."

"Is it actually made of silver?" Seth hadn't wanted to get involved in the conversation, but he couldn't help himself. Who paid that sort of money for a pram? It was almost enough to buy the cheapest new car on the market and it was ridiculous.

"It's called the Aston Martin edition and I saw one when Nath took me up to London and we had a browse round the baby department in Harrods." Daisy shot him another one of her looks. "We only want the best for our baby. You wouldn't understand, Seth, seeing as you can't even keep a relationship going for nine months, let alone commit to starting a family."

"You're right and it's none of my business. Pretend I'm not here."

"Hmm." Daisy was clearly thinking she'd been right all along to ask him to leave, but it would have been even more awkward if he'd got up and left at that point.

"Okay, so do you need all of the money you invested back?" Ben cut through the tension by getting to the bottom line.

"Yes, ideally, the whole forty thousand. I know it might take you a bit of time to get the money together, but you should be able to re-mortgage the flat now if you need to, it must have gone up in value quite a bit."

"Of course, and I'll work out the increase in your share when I pay you back." Ben kept his voice level and Seth could almost see his mind whirring; wondering how he was going to pay Daisy back and still manage to invest in the farm.

"Don't be daft, Benji. I don't want any interest." Daisy laid a hand over her brother's. "Call any increase in the investment my wedding present to you and Ellie."

"Thank you, that's really generous. But we'll see how much it is, because we can't accept it if it's thousands of pounds"

"Nonsense! I couldn't think of a better wedding gift!" Daisy smiled and relaxed back into her chair, rubbing her bump. She wasn't to know that it was about the worse pre-wedding news she could have given Ben, with the financial worries he and Ellie already had. Now Seth's mind was whirring as well, there had to be some way he could help his old friend out. He just had to work out how and find a solution that Ben would accept too.

Chapter Five

Friday morning started earlier than expected for Olivia. If she wanted to get over her jet lag as quickly as possible and adjust to a new time zone, she'd come to the right place. Ellie and Karen had done wonders since taking over the farm, but the renovations they'd completed on the farmhouse had been sympathetic. As a result, there were no double-glazed UPVC windows to spoil the character, or keep out the sound of Gerald, and the farm's resident cockerel, trying their best to out-sing each other. It was like being caught between Alfie Boe and Katherine Jenkins in full voice, only a lot less tuneful.

Olivia looked at her watch; five thirty a.m. Peering out of the window, it was already a beautiful sunny morning and she could just make out Ellie walking down towards the bottom paddock with a bucket. Her best friend had certainly taken to country life. They'd shared a Chinese takeaway with Ben and Seth the night before to celebrate Olivia's new job. They'd stayed up talking after the boys had gone back to Ben's flat above the surgery and it had been well after midnight before they'd finally headed up to bed. So, if Ellie could be up – looking remarkably energetic – then Olivia could too. She glanced in the mirror. Well maybe not energetic, but she could at least get dressed and head outside to help out.

Ellie was filling up the water trough in the donkey's paddock when Olivia came up behind her, making her drop the hose. "Morning."

"You nearly gave me a heart attack!"

"Sorry. Maybe I should have whistled so you knew I was coming."

"I just wasn't expecting to see you up so early." She patted the donkey nearest her, who lifted his head for a moment and then returned to eating the pad of hay in front of him. "I'm guessing Gerald's morning sing-song might have had something to do with it."

"Well he certainly knows how to get attention." The sun was already warm on Olivia's face and she was glad the donkey had woken her up. She could taste the salt on her lips, a light breeze carrying it up from the sea, and she didn't want to miss a minute lying in bed. It might have been different if it had been a grey day and the sea had been lashing the cliff face. Although, on a day like this, it was hard to imagine that ever happening, even though she knew only too well that the English weather could change in a heartbeat.

"Gerald has always known how to get exactly what he wants. Give me a minute and we can head back to the house, so I can whip us up some breakfast."

"Don't be daft, I've come out to help. Just tell me what you want me to do."

"I could get used to having you around, you know." Ellie nudged her and Gerald looked up again to see what all the fuss was about.

"Shall I start by letting the chickens out into their run?"

"That would be brilliant, but are you sure? I know what you're like with birds."

"Like I said before, I'm getting better all the time. I went to the farm at the school yesterday and I managed not to run in the other direction when I realised they had a couple of ducks there!"

"Okay, well there's a basket by the side of the run and you can put any eggs they've laid in there. I just need to check on the fencing in the paddock the sheep are in, as I can't sleep at night when the wind's blowing, in case we lose part of the fence and the sheep end up toppling over the cliff! It's becoming a bit of an obsession of mine to check on the fence every day."

"Shall I feed Dolly or something whilst you're doing that?" Olivia suspected that the heavily pregnant goat, who was due to give birth any day now, was another reason Ellie was up so early.

"Yes, there's a bucket of feed made up for her in the store room next to the stable she's in, but she needs some new bedding put down. You can just tie her up outside to have her breakfast and I'll sort the bedding when I'm done with the fence. If you're sure you're okay with that?"

"I'm still getting to grips with this country life, but I remember everything your Aunt Hilary taught me and I think I can handle the chickens and Dolly. Although I'll be keeping a firm grip on her, given how good she's been at escaping in the past."

"She usually just follows the food. We took her to an animal blessing service at the church and she ate the order of service right out of the vicar's hands! So, as long as you've got her breakfast in a bucket, she'll be totally loyal to you." Ellie grinned at her. "Who'd have thought we'd give up those dreams of a penthouse flat to be mucking out goats and donkeys instead?"

"There's nowhere I'd rather be." Olivia gave her friend a quick hug. Ellie wasn't going to need any pre-wedding crash diets, there wasn't an ounce of fat on her, which was hardly surprising with everything she had to do.

Leaving Ellie to finish feeding the donkeys, Olivia was determined not to let her friend down and she strode purposefully towards the chicken coop. Chickens had always scared her, even before her bird phobia got really out-of-hand. The way they moved and pecked at the ground and sometimes each other, made her nervous. One of the boys who'd lived in The Copse had kept a pet goose and it had taken to attacking the other kids when they walked up to his end of the road. It was what had started Olivia's phobia, although it was probably an exaggeration to call it that. She had absolutely no problem with birds if they stayed where they belonged – up in the sky or perched high on a branch – it was just when she had to deal with them at close proximity that she could feel her pulse quicken and the desire to run in the opposite direction kick in.

"Out you go girls." Olivia opened a door in the chicken coop, so that the chickens could wander down the slope to the run. The cockerel was in his own run next door and Ellie must have already let him out, as he was strutting around the place and ruffling his feathers trying to impress the girls living next door. A couple of the chickens weren't too keen to leave their beds and Olivia closed her eyes as she gently put her hands underneath them to lift them up and shoo them out. She was okay if she didn't see their beady eyes. She could still remember how much it hurt when the goose had attacked her, but it hadn't been as bad as the boys laughing at her and making honking noises for weeks after she'd been the first to be attacked. It might not have been charitable, but she'd actually been relieved when the goose had eventually got around to attacking almost everyone else. At least it had stopped her being singled out as *'goose girl'*.

With the chickens safely in their run, she collected the eggs, a still-warm collection of white, brown and speckled eggs that seemed to epitomise country life. Arriving at Dolly's stable, the scene wasn't quite so idyllic. The goat's pendulous belly swayed from side to side as she walked over to the stable door and Ellie hadn't been wrong when she'd said Daisy's bedding would need changing. If she was going to be of any use on the farm, Olivia couldn't just stick to the easy jobs. Tying Dolly up to the fence, as Ellie had instructed, she gave the goat her breakfast and began to load up a wheelbarrow with the old bedding.

"Are you sure you haven't had a party in here? It looks like there's been a whole herd of goats hanging out."

"Do you always talk to the animals?" Ellie appeared around the stable door, as Olivia loaded up the wheelbarrow for the third time.

"Only when I think no-one is watching me!"

"That makes two of us then." Ellie picked up another pitchfork. "Are you sure I can't persuade you to give up teaching and work here full time?"

"It wouldn't take a lot to convince me, but I think I'd miss the kids too much."

"The offers always there, if you ever change your mind. At least it will be if I can get some more bookings for the winter." Olivia was grateful Ellie didn't try too hard to persuade her. It would have been so easy to hide out on the farm, but it wasn't what she wanted. They finished the clean-up of Dolly's stable, passing the time in easy conversation about everything and nothing. Just as they always had. It was something else Olivia was grateful for; that her time away hadn't really changed anything between them.

"Aren't you glad we spent all that time giving her a luxurious bed?" Ellie grinned at Olivia, when Dolly started to eat her bedding as soon as she was let back into her stable.

"Well she is eating for two." She followed Ellie, as she pushed the wheelbarrow away from the stable block. Only looking up when she heard a shout, she nearly cannoned into Ellie, who'd promptly set the wheelbarrow down.

"Isn't that your mum and Alan?" They definitely didn't seem the type of couple to be out for an early morning jog, but there was no denying it was Ellie's parents running towards them.

"Oh Ellie, Liv, thank goodness you're already up." Karen was puffing so much by the time she drew level with them that she could hardly get her words out.

"Mum, what on earth's the matter?"

"It's The Old Hop Kiln, it's burnt down!" Karen's arms flew up into the air as she spoke and Olivia tried to work out what was going on. As far she knew, Alan didn't have a hop kiln on his farm.

"Is anyone hurt?" Ellie's eyes widened as she spoke.

"No, thank God. It started in the kitchen, but the damage is so bad it's looking as if it's going to need a complete rebuild."

"That's awful, but you could have just called me, instead of half-killing yourself running over here to tell me."

"No, you don't understand..." Karen still couldn't get the words out quickly enough, so Alan stepped in.

"They've got a surprise pearl wedding anniversary booked in for this evening and there are guests coming from as far away as Spain to attend, but now the poor family have got no venue." Alan was looking as devastated as he might if it had been his own party. Ellie was right, he was a very nice man and exactly the sort of husband Karen deserved.

"The Old Hop Kiln is a restaurant and party venue on the other side of Kelsea Bay." Ellie turned to Olivia to explain. "It's pretty much our only competition around here for summer parties, but this is the last thing I'd want to happen to anyone."

"Do you think we could help, with the pearl wedding party I mean?" Karen gave her daughter a beseeching look.

"Of course." Ellie was already nodding and Olivia wondered if she was hearing right.

"Haven't you got a wedding tomorrow and a baby shower on Sunday? How on earth are you going to fit that in too?"

"I don't know, but we will." Ellie shrugged, although the look in her eyes gave away the panic she must have been feeling.

"We've done it before. When Ben's sister got married here, we had to redo all the flowers and the wedding cake with a couple of hours to spare, after the animals got loose." Alan put a reassuring arm around his step-daughter's shoulders as he spoke.

"They were having outside caterers for the party, so at least the food's taken care of. We can get some of the casual staff in to run the bar and The Old Hop Kiln will send up their waiting staff, plus there's a band booked, so it's really only the setting up and the venue décor to do." Karen sounded as if she was trying to convince herself.

"But weren't you going to spend today setting up for the wedding?" It wasn't that Olivia didn't want to help out, she just couldn't see how it could all be done.

"Yes, but like I said we'll manage somehow." Ellie gave her a wry smile. "After all, we'd want someone to do the same for us, wouldn't we?"

"We would, but I doubt many people would do what you're doing." Olivia returned her smile. "And that's why I love you all so much. Just tell me what I need to do to help and I'll do it."

As Karen and Ellie started running through the to-do list, Olivia relaxed her shoulders. It was going to be a long and very busy weekend, but if anyone could pull it off the Chapmans could and she was willing to do whatever it took to help. If she'd had any idea what that promise would get her in to, she might have kept quiet.

****

Decorating the barn for the party was going well. Seth had got back from his interview with Peter Coleman and was going to be starting at the summer school on Monday alongside Olivia. Alan had mustered help from a few of the local farm hands, along with some of the casual staff who worked at the wedding venue and who were willing to work an extra shift. Alan soon had them organised like a military unit. Gwyneth and Paul, who were the couple celebrating thirty years together, had apparently met at a blues club, where Gwyneth had worked behind the bar and Paul had joined as a doorman shortly after he'd first arrived from Jamaica. Sally, their daughter, who was arranging the surprise party, had asked if The Old Hop Kiln could dress the venue as much like a blues club as possible. So when a piano turned up on the back of flatbed truck, it took all of Alan's organisational skills to get it manoeuvred into the barn. Olivia didn't even want to think about how they'd get it out again and re-dress the barn in the pink and grey theme the bride had chosen for the wedding the next day.

"There's a singer and pianist coming along to provide the entertainment tonight." Ellie briefly looked up from laying one of the tables, her face almost as red as the confetti hearts she was sprinkling on the linen table cloths. They were all hot and tired, but everyone was working really hard to make sure that Gwyneth and Paul's big night went according to plan, despite everything. Thankfully the decorations for the party hadn't been inside The Old Hop Kiln when the fire broke out.

"Did their daughter say how she's planning to get them here? I suppose it would have been a bit easier at The Old Hop Kiln, as it's a restaurant, but they might suspect something when she brings them up to the farm." Olivia filled up a bowl with personalised Love Heart sweets, which were stamped with Gwyneth and Paul's names and the date of their wedding.

"Apparently she told them she's ordered a cake from Mum to take to the restaurant. As far as they know, they're just meeting Sally's brothers there for a little get together. They've got no idea there's going be over a hundred guests here. We can get everyone to park on the other side of the farmhouse, so it doesn't give the game away at the last minute. When Sally told me what her mum has been through, I was more determined than ever to get it right."

"She definitely deserves to be pampered." Olivia folded the napkins the way Ellie had shown her. They wouldn't win any awards, but her table wouldn't completely let the side down either. Gwyneth's daughter had explained to Ellie on the phone that three years earlier her mother had suffered a virus which had resulted in unexplained paralysis, and for a long time they didn't think she'd recover. But with intensive physiotherapy and unrelenting support from her husband, she was finally on the mend. The highlight of the evening was going to be a performance of their song – Etta James' *'At Last.'* It had already been an old song when the couple met, but Sally said it was a favourite of the singer who'd regularly performed at the blues club and it had been the first song they'd ever danced to. Gwyneth had listened to the song all the time during her recovery, according to Sally, and her one wish had been to be able to dance with her husband again. The anniversary party was their chance to make that wish come true.

Ellie's mobile rang again and she raised her eyebrows. "This better not be any more unexpected news, I don't think my blood pressure can take it. I'm already so hot that I feel like taking a dip in Gerald's water trough just to cool off."

Olivia carried on creating slightly lopsided napkin arrangements as she listened to Ellie's side of the phone conversation. It didn't sound like good news.

"You're not going to believe this!" Ellie's face had gone from bright red to deathly pale in less than thirty seconds.

"That was Denise from The Old Hop Kiln. Apparently, the singer and pianist they'd booked for tonight have been in a car crash. He's got whiplash and she's got a fractured wrist, so obviously they've cancelled the gig. Denise has spent the last hour ringing round to try and get a replacement, but with it being the height of holiday season she hasn't even been able to find a mobile DJ who's available.

"Oh no!" Poor Sally, she'd put her heart and soul into organising this party for her parents and it was just one thing after another going wrong. What next? An outbreak of listeria at the catering company? At this rate, they'd all be listening to the radio and ordering take away pizza.

"What's up?" Ben spoke as he and Seth made their way across from the other side of the barn.

"The blues singer and pianist they'd booked for tonight have had an accident and there's no one free to stand in for them. I know it's not the biggest problem in the world, but, as far as tonight's party goes, it's a disaster."

"Seth can play the piano." Ben looked at his best friend and Seth shook his head.

"I mean, I can play a bit, but I'm far from being a professional."

"And we're far from being able to be picky." Ben slapped him on the back. "Anyway, you virtually paid your way through uni playing piano in that Chinese restaurant."

"That was background music, not the main entertainment and I certainly can't sing. Didn't you say it was an Etta James song they wanted? It'll take some singer to pull that off."

"Liv, you used to love singing. You were in all those productions at school and with that theatre group for years..." Ellie looked in her direction and Olivia realised she'd been holding her breath, waiting for her friend to suggest she sang. It had been years since she'd performed anywhere other than a karaoke bar, where no one really expected you to be any good. Seth was right, it would take a really good singer to pull off an Etta James song and it wasn't something she even wanted to try.

"I haven't sung properly since I was at university and I'm no more qualified to perform in front of a crowd than any of the rest of you. There must be someone else who can do it?" Seth was nodding along. They were being railroaded into something neither of them wanted to do, but for once she was going to stand her ground. The alternative was just too terrifying to think about.

"You could play the song if you had the music though, couldn't you?" Ben clearly wasn't going to let Seth out of it that easily. He and Ellie made quite a team.

"Technically I could play anything if I had the music, but it doesn't mean it's going to be any good."

"Well, if we had the luxury of worrying about it being really good, we would. Please Seth, it means so much to the family." Ellie was virtually pleading and Seth had no chance against the pincer movement she and Ben had performed on him.

"Just don't expect me to say yes, even if Seth does." Olivia had a sudden urge to cry. This wasn't fair. She'd lost her enthusiasm for a lot of things when she'd been in Australia, burying herself in work and not much else. She wasn't even sure if she *could* sing anymore.

"Thank you so much for doing this!" A stunning looking woman in her twenties, with dark corkscrew curls, had walked into the barn. Carrying balloons spelling out the words 'mum and dad', she looked like a young Halle Berry and half the staff stopped what they were doing to stare at her.

"You must be, Sally? I'm Ellie, we spoke on the phone earlier." Ellie took the balloons from her and passed them to one of the bar staff who tied them up near the piano.

"That's right. You're an absolute life safer!" Sally looked around the barn and smiled. "I thought the night was going to be ruined when we got that call from The Old Hop Kiln, but if I'd known how lovely it was here, I've have booked this place from the start. My grandmother has put together a photo board of Mum and Dad's life together over the years, if there's somewhere we can display that too? She's just 'supervising' my granddad, insisting he carries it out from the car, instead of letting me do it!"

"No problem at all. We can display it over by the table where the cake will be cut later, if you think that would work?" Ellie smiled as Sally nodded her head, but Olivia knew her well enough to read the expression on her face. If only everything could have been solved as easily.

"That's brilliant! I can't believe how well it's all coming together. I thought I was going to cry this morning when I found out about the restaurant. Olivia dug her nails into her palm, feeling guilty. She might have felt like crying when Ellie suggested she sing, but she was absolutely certain Sally would cry when she heard the entertainment she'd worked so hard to plan for her parents was off.

"Oh Granddad, I told you I should have brought that in!" Sally virtually had to wrestle the photo board away from the man, who Olivia couldn't see behind it.

"Just because he's got arthritis, he's perfectly capable of a bit of light lifting!" The last time Olivia had heard that voice the woman had been in a panic about her dog, but Sally's grandmother wasn't panicking now. Hetty's face changed as she stopped nagging Bert and looked around the barn. "Oh Sally, you are a clever girl, your mum's going to love this!"

"It's nothing to do with me, it's all down to Ellie and her team." Sally looked as if she was going to throw her arms around them all and Ellie's sigh was audible, the strained smile melting from her face.

"I'm really sorry to tell you this, but we've just had a call to say that the singer and pianist you've booked have been in a minor car accident. Thankfully neither of them are badly hurt, but they aren't going to be able to make it tonight."

"Thank goodness it wasn't more serious." Even as Sally tried to be upbeat, Olivia could see tears weren't far away. "I'd ask for a stiff drink, if I wasn't driving. If things come in threes, I'm wondering what's going to happen next."

"Don't you know anyone who could stand in?" Hetty looked towards Ben. "You must know loads of people as a vet and you were absolutely brilliant when Casper got knocked over."

"Well, I do know someone, but I'm not sure they'd be up for it, because it's a long time since they sang in front of an audience." Ben's gaze slid towards Olivia, but he quickly looked away again, trying not to make it obvious who he was looking at.

"It's only really that one song we need." Sally's eyes had filled with tears now. She was less forceful than her grandmother, but her words had even more impact. "I don't care if we have to play CDs for the rest of the night, but that's their song and we've all been through hell not knowing if she'd even make it to tonight."

"Could you at least ask your friend?" Hetty moved to stand in front of Ben, looking as if she might be prepared to block his path until he did.

"Well..." This time Ben looked straight at Seth.

"Okay, I'll do it, but only if Olivia does it with me."

"Don't put it all on me!"

"Are you the singer?" Bert turned towards her and laid his hand on her arm. "Beautiful and talented too. Not only that but she makes an excellent cup of tea."

"I used to sing. A bit." Olivia looked down at her shoes. If she made eye contact with Sally or Bert she'd fold and agree to do something that filled her with dread. Worst still, if she caught Hetty's steely gaze, she might find herself agreeing to sing for the whole evening.

"She's being far too modest. Olivia's got a great voice, she used to sing all the time and I'm sure she could more than pull this off." Ellie had the good sense not to look at her as she spoke. She loved Ellie like a sister, but sometimes she acted like one, dropping her in it in a way that only family could get away with.

"I just don't think I'll do it justice."

"Please Liv, you know I'd do it if I could hold a single note, but you must remember that time in Spain when the bar owner said he'd give me a free jug of sangria to stop singing, because I was driving customers away."

"Yes, I remember." She couldn't help laughing at the memory. Ellie was brilliant at lots things, but singing wasn't one of them. When they'd had that holiday together, before they went to university in different parts of the country, it had created lots of memories, but that night had stuck in her mind.

"You know why you're our only hope then?"

"And you know why I'm never going to forgive you for making me do this?"

"I'll take it on the chin for Gwyneth and Paul." Ellie screwed up her face. "So, you'll do it then?" Against her better judgement, Olivia found herself nodding as Ellie flung her arms around her. Quickly followed by Sally and then Bert, which earned him another one of Hetty's looks, but then even she smiled at Olivia.

"Thank you so much, this will make their evening." Hetty's face softened further and she slipped her hand into Bert's. They might bicker, but there was clearly a lot of love in their family. Who was she to stand in the way of their planned celebrations?

"Just don't expect too much."

"That's settled then and you two are released from decorating duties straight away." Ellie finally offered her an apologetic smile. "You'd better get some practice in."

Ellie and Ben took the family off to set up the photo board, before Olivia had the chance to change her mind.

"Is there no end to your talent? A stand-in riding instructor and now a pianist?" If she sounded annoyed with Seth then he'd have to live with it. It was at least partly his fault for getting her into this, if he hadn't backed down first, they might still have got out of it.

"Some might say that I'm a jack of all trades and a master of none, but what else could we do?" There was such an earnest look in his green eyes that she couldn't stay angry with him for long.

"Do you think they'll notice if I mime?"

"I think so." Seth gave her hand a squeeze. "You'll be fine and what's the worst that can happen? It's not like they can sack us from a job we never asked for in the first place."

"We could ruin Gwyneth and Paul's big night though."

"Put it this way, it'll be memorable whatever happens. Even if we're a disaster, they'll get a laugh out of it and they'll never forget it."

"I'd like to say that's a comfort, but I'm not going to lie!"

"It'll all be over by tomorrow. As my old Nan used to say when life was going through a rough patch, this too shall pass."

"There is that." Olivia smiled despite herself. It was a thought she'd clung to during her darkest days in Australia. She'd survived everything Josh had put her through, so humiliating herself in front of a room full of strangers suddenly didn't seem quite so bad. As Seth had said, what was the worst that could happen?

****

"Right are you ready?" Seth looked at her and she shook her head so quickly her long blonde ponytail whipped from side-to-side.

"I'm never going to be ready." Olivia's hands were shaking, but Seth looked as if he did this sort of thing every day. "And you're not helping, you're far better at playing the piano than you let on earlier." They'd been practising all afternoon and had gone over to the house to get ready once the party kicked off. It had been nerve wracking enough for Olivia to sing in front of her friends and the staff who had still been busy setting up the room, but now they were about to deliver the long-awaited performance. Ben had managed to borrow an old mobile disco unit from the caravan park next door, as they'd upgraded their system at the beginning of the summer, but there was no DJ to operate it. So, he'd had to learn how to cue up tracks on his laptop and play them through the system. At least it meant Olivia and Seth were only performing one song, but that was more than enough.

"When I was staying with my grandparents, my granddad used to earn extra money singing and playing piano in the working men's clubs around the East End where they lived. It was more Chas and Dave than the Blues, but he taught me how to play and it stood me in good stead when I was at uni. It was a much better way of earning a bit of beer money than delivering pizzas for minimum wage like poor old Ben had to." Seth turned her to face him. "Anyway, I don't want to hear any more about you not being able to sing. You've got a fantastic voice."

"Let's just get it over and done with then, shall we?" Standing so close to Seth she wasn't sure if she felt better or worse. Looking at his face was a nice distraction, but the sudden desire to lean forward and rest her head on his chest took her by surprise. She just wanted *someone* to lean on, that was all.

"Try and enjoy it if you can." Seth laughed at the expression that must have crossed her face.

Stepping into the room, it wasn't just Olivia's hands that were shaking, her legs felt like they didn't want to hold her up either and it was only when Seth placed a hand in the small of her back that she realised she'd stopped moving altogether.

It was a bit like an out of body experience, when she stepped up on to the mobile staging Ellie and her team had set up. Ben faded out the song he'd been playing and Olivia bit her lip hard, gripping the microphone stand to hold her up. As Seth played the first few bars of the song, for a second or two she seriously considered bolting off the stage and not stopping until she got to her parents' place in Yorkshire. She missed her cue, but it didn't seem to faze Seth, who just repeated the introduction. And then she started to sing and it was like someone else had taken over, she sang the first few lines staring straight down at the microphone, but when she finally looked up, she realised she and Seth had caught the audience's attention. Most of them were still seated around the tables that lined the edges of the room surrounding the dancefloor, but there were a few people only a couple of feet away from her, swaying in time to the song. She looked down again, desperate not to accidently make eye contact with anyone who might put her off her stride. Especially if it was Ellie or Karen; she could just about get through this if she pretended she was on her own at home, singing into her hairbrush.

She opened her eyes again just in time to see Sally gently guiding her parents to the dancefloor. Gwyneth was still a bit unsteady on her feet, but she leant against Paul's chest as the guests began to cheer. Olivia had goose pimples; a love story was playing out in front of her eyes and everyone else seemed to be feeling it too.

Ben was getting the hang of DJ'ing and as Olivia belted out the final lines, he had the next song cued up to go straight away and no-one seemed in any rush to leave the dancefloor.

"That was amazing! See I told you." Seth stood up as Olivia walked across the stage to meet him and took hold of her arms, so that she had to stop and look up at him again.

"I feel like I've run a marathon!" She laughed, flooded with the sort of relief that only comes when something you've really dreaded is out of the way.

"You're a star."

"Hardly but thank you for getting me through it." Leaning forward, she kissed him. She'd had every intention of pecking him on the cheek - a friendly thank you - but instead she gently brushed her lips against his before pulling away. Scanning the room to see if anyone, especially Ellie, had been watching them, Olivia was relieved to see everyone transfixed by Gwyneth and Paul, who were still on the dancefloor. "Sorry." She whispered the words to Seth, who shook his head.

"Don't be, that's quite possibly the best thank you I've ever had."

"Thank God that was a one-off performance!" She laughed again, more to fill the silence than anything. He was probably trying to work out if she meant the singing or the kiss. Trouble was, she wasn't even sure herself.

Chapter Six

Saturday passed in a blur. Olivia and Ellie were up before Gerald and the cockerel even had the chance to start their morning duet and wake everyone up. Seth and Ben were at the farm just after six, at the same time as Karen and Alan walked over from his farm next door. There was no time for her to talk to Seth or Ellie properly. What would she have said anyway? That she wasn't sure why she'd kissed him? Some things were better left unsaid, put down to the heat of the moment and the sheer relief at having got through something she'd been dreading.

The wedding was catering for fewer guests than the party the night before, but there were more arriving for the evening. It meant that both the gazebo and the barn had to be dressed and ready. Olivia offered to help out in the bar at the evening reception and it was after one a.m. before she got back to her room at the farmhouse, kicked off her shoes and set the alarm, knowing that she had to be up at six the next morning to start all over again. How Ellie kept it going all summer long she didn't know, although even she'd admitted that agreeing to host the anniversary party had put a lot more pressure on than normal.

Sunday morning was another bright day and the light streaming through the window beat both Gerald and the alarm clock to wake her up. It was just after half past five and she needed coffee if she was going to get through the day. Hopefully a baby shower wouldn't be as demanding as the wedding, and at least no one would expect her to burst into song. Still, there were sixty people coming, so it was going to be another busy day.

"Morning." Olivia was surprised to see Ellie and Karen already in the kitchen, icing row upon row of cupcakes and topping them with sugar paper daisies.

“Oh Liv, I didn’t get a chance to tell you yesterday but you had me in tears singing on Friday night.” Karen gave Olivia a powerful hug, without ever letting go of her piping bag.

“What, it was so bad it brought tears to your eyes?”

“Don’t be silly. It was beautiful, you should never have given up singing.” Karen was already back to icing cakes at a rate that could have qualified for interest from the Guinness Book of Records. It would have taken Olivia about an hour to do each cake and, even then, it would probably look like someone had sat on them.

“I have to admit I enjoyed it more than I thought I would.”

“Yes, I noticed.” Ellie looked up from sticking another flower to the icing and grinned at Olivia. Had she seen the kiss after all? Either way, Olivia wasn’t going to say anything. Maybe if she didn’t make a big thing of it, then Ellie wouldn’t either.

“I can’t believe you’re both up and about already. I didn’t think today was going to be quite so hectic? Does anyone want another drink?” There was a pot of coffee on the side and Olivia poured herself one when the others shook their heads.

“It wouldn’t normally be, but Daisy likes things ‘just so’.” Karen pulled a face. “Ben’s sister is a lovely girl, but she’s quite… demanding.”

“What Mum means is that she’s a bit of a diva!” Ellie laughed. “This is her second party for the baby and it’s still a month until he’s even due. She had a gender reveal a few months back.”

“A gender reveal?”

“Yes, Mum was given an envelope from the sonographer which Daisy and her husband hadn’t seen, revealing that the baby’s a boy. Mum had to bake a cake for them to cut at the party, the inside of which revealed the gender of the baby to everyone there, so obviously it had to have a blue sponge.”

“Do people really do things like that?” Olivia took a sip of her coffee, it all sounded a bit over the top to her.

"Daisy does. It was good fun, actually, but I'm not sure it's something I'd want to do." Ellie turned her attention back to the cakes and Olivia found herself wondering how long it would be before her friend thought about having a child of her own.

"Shall I go down and feed the animals, or is there anything else you want me to do here?"

"That would be brilliant, if you're sure you don't mind?" Ellie was working on her next cake and a horrible realisation suddenly struck Olivia. They'd planned a trip in a high-speed boat for the hen and stag party, but she'd forgotten all about Ben's sister being eight months pregnant. She'd have to speak to Seth; they'd need to think of something else and quickly too. She wasn't about to worry Ellie with it though.

"That's fine, I'll come back up to the house when I've finished sorting them all out and see what I can do to help."

"If we're not here, we'll be down at the barn." Ellie stopped decorating the cupcakes and looked up at her again. "I don't know what we ever did around here without you. Don't disappear again too soon, will you?"

"I've got no plans to go anywhere for now. Except to give Gerald his breakfast before he comes and helps himself to some cupcakes!" It was true, she was in no rush to leave. Maybe she should be spending more time thinking about her next career move, or where she was going to live after the wedding. But they were problems for another day, there were hungry animals to feed and that was a much easier problem to solve.

****

"I thought I might find you down here, doing a Snow White and singing to the animals!" Seth leant over the five-bar gate as Olivia filled up the donkeys' water trough and flicked a stream of water in his direction, making him jump back out of the way.

"You should never insult a woman when she's got a hosepipe in her hand, not unless you want to end up soaking wet!"

"No insult intended. In fact, I'd love to hear you sing again. But for now, I've come down here to see what I can do to help you. It was a choice between mucking out the goat and helping make daisy-themed paperchains for the baby shower, so there was no choice really."

"Oh, there is an end to your talents then. Art and crafts not your thing?"

"Daisy's parties aren't my thing."

"I'd forgotten that you must know her quite well. So, you never had a crush on your best friend's big sister then?" Olivia kept her tone casual, but for some reason she wanted to know the answer, and she was hoping he'd say no. The thought of Seth suffering unrequited love for Daisy – or, worse still, dating her – bothered Olivia, even though it made absolutely no sense.

"I was eighteen when we first met, when Ben and I had just started uni together, so I was getting a bit old for schoolboy crushes, and I quickly worked out that the person Daisy was most interested in was Daisy."

"In that case I don't think she's going to be impressed that we forgot all about her being pregnant when we decided to book the seal trip for the stag and hen day. Do you think we'll be able to cancel it?" As Olivia spoke, Gerald nudged her, the old donkey keen to see if she was hiding any treats. She had a handful of pony nuts stuffed into her jeans' pocket and she pulled out a few to feed him.

"It's fine. Daisy has already told me she won't be able to make the hen party. I know from experience that Daisy doesn't really do parties that don't revolve around Daisy."

"Sounds like there's a lot more to that story."

"It was Ben's twenty-first birthday when I saw it for the first time. She created a real drama about the cake being bigger than the one she'd had for her twenty-first and it could have ruined the night if we'd let it." Seth shrugged. "She's good hearted really, but she just likes being the centre of attention. I mean who has a baby shower that isn't baby-themed, but covered in daisies instead, so no one forgets who the most important person is?"

"Well, I suppose it's her last chance to be the centre of attention before the baby comes along and becomes everyone's priority."

"Hmm." Seth raised an eyebrow. "Enough about Daisy. What do you want me to do to help? I'm all yours." It was a throw away comment, but there was an awkward pause as she concentrated on studying Gerald's mane before she could look at him. It would be a shame if her moment's madness in kissing him made things uncomfortable between them.

"Well you did mention a desire to muck out Dolly's stable." She smiled at the look that crossed his face. "She needs your expertise anyway. I can't believe she hasn't given birth yet, she looks fit to pop, and you'd be a much better judge than me about whether she's okay or not."

"Ben's your man for that job. I know more about tigers than I do about goats. The goats I do come into contact with are usually the big cats' dinner, so they're way beyond even the most talented vet's help!"

"Maybe I won't let you near Dolly then! That's one way of getting out of clearing out the stable, who'd have thought Daisy wasn't the only diva around here?" She couldn't help laughing at his look of mock indignation.

"A diva?" He grinned, opening the five-bar gate for her, just as a squawking seagull decided to see if Gerald and the other donkeys had left any of their breakfast. The whoosh of air, as it swooped down, made it feel as if it was only inches above

Olivia's head and she dropped her bucket in shock, her bird phobia kicking in and sending her flying into Seth.

"Sorry."

"I'm not." He looked at her for a long moment and half of her wanted to kiss him again, whilst the other half wanted to run. Hadn't she said that the absolute last thing she wanted was another relationship? Especially a long distance one. Either way, she wasn't going to be the one to make another move.

"Right, well Dolly won't clean up her own stable unfortunately. I'll get to that, if you can check the fencing in the sheep paddock and then let the chickens out?"

She picked up her bucket and headed towards Dolly's stable before he even had the chance to answer her, wondering if she could walk as quickly as she was and still kick herself at the same time. What on earth was she thinking even contemplating being more than friends with Seth? She tried to picture Josh for a moment and remember why she had sworn off new relationships, but all she could picture when she closed her eyes was Seth smiling. Which wasn't helpful at all.

****

By the time everyone was assembled for Daisy's baby shower, Olivia had convinced herself that she was overthinking everything as usual. She was only human and just because she liked Seth, it didn't mean she had to do anything about it. At best, he was giving out mixed signals and she'd been through far too much to play those sorts of games.

Ellie had insisted that she attend the baby shower, even though she'd never met Daisy but she felt more comfortable helping out the waiting staff. Daisy and her friends and family were busy playing games like *'guess-the-baby-food'*, which Olivia was more than happy to miss out on, and passing around a book to fill-out with messages for Daisy, her husband Nathan, and the baby. There was also a *'guess-the-baby-name'* quiz, but everything else was Daisy themed, from the cupcakes that

Karen and Ellie had been preparing from dawn, to the edible ox-eye daisies floating in glasses of champagne, or sparkling elderberry for Daisy and anyone else only wanting a soft drink.

"So, you must be the famous Olivia I've heard so much about." Daisy smiled at her warmly, as Olivia topped up her drink. "I'm so glad you were able to step in for chief bridesmaid duties." She rubbed her stomach and Olivia smiled to herself. It was subtle one-up-man-ship, letting Olivia know that the only reason she was chief bridesmaid was because Daisy didn't want the job while she was so heavily pregnant.

"Lovely to meet you at last and I was really pleased to be able to step in." Daisy didn't need to know that it was a promise she and Ellie had made to each other when they were about eight years old.

"I did try to persuade Benji and Ellie to put the wedding off until after I've had the baby and got back into shape, but they just can't wait to get married!" Daisy sounded genuinely delighted that her little brother was so obviously in love, despite it thwarting her plans. Seth was right, she definitely wasn't *all* bad.

"I'll try and live up to the job, but if you've got any advice, since you know Ben so much better than I do, I'd be more than happy to hear it."

"I'm not really in a position to give advice." Daisy rubbed her belly again. "I've never actually been a bridesmaid before, but you've already been a bridesmaid at Karen and Alan's wedding, haven't you?"

"It was great fun, but Ellie was in charge of everything, so I just had to turn up really."

"It was such a shame we missed their wedding, but we'd just found out about the baby and Nathan took me to New York for Christmas to celebrate. We knew it would be the last chance to do something like that before our little one comes along." For some reason, Daisy seemed to want to let her know that she'd had an invite to Karen and Alan's wedding. Maybe she wasn't as confident as she looked, it certainly felt like she had something to prove. "You should be careful, though, not to take on any more bridesmaid duties. What is it they say, three times a bridesmaid never a bride?"

"This will be my fourth time, actually. I did it a couple of times for family members when I was younger."

"Oh." For a moment Daisy didn't seem to know what to say and Olivia felt like laughing. Did she really believe old wives' tales like that meant anything? "From what Ben and Seth have said, you're quite the career girl anyway and not interested in all that. So, I don't suppose it matters, even if it wasn't just a silly old saying."

"Yes, well have a lovely afternoon. I've got a bit of work to do before starting my new job tomorrow, so I'm going to head off soon, but I'm sure I'll see you in the run up to the wedding."

"Absolutely and good luck with the new job!" Daisy was already turning towards one of her friends, as Olivia scooped up some empty champagne glasses. Of course, she wasn't bothered by being a bridesmaid for the fourth time and Daisy was right, getting married wasn't the be-all-and-end-all. It didn't even make her list of hopes right now. But Daisy discussing Olivia with Ben and Seth was what bothered her, and the fact they all seemed to have written her off on the relationship front. Maybe it wasn't surprising; after all, hadn't she done that herself?

****

"We can't keep bumping into each other like this." Seth was already leaning on Dolly's stable door when Olivia went to check on the goat, on her way back to the farmhouse.

"I just wanted to see if she was okay." Olivia's face flushed. Now she knew he'd been discussing her with Daisy, she felt more awkward around him than she had before. As if they'd all been judging her.

"She's in labour."

"Oh, wow, really? I thought you didn't know anything about goats. Should I go and get Ben?"

"No, I'm sure he's enjoying listening to Daisy and her friends talking about childbirth." Seth smiled. If only he wasn't so disarming when he did, it would all be much easier. "Anyway, Dolly's doing a great job and there's no need for anyone to intervene unless it looks like she's getting into trouble."

They stood, mostly in companionable silence, as Dolly delivered three kids, without needing anyone's help, and Olivia instantly fell in love with the little black-and-white bundles who were soon on their feet and feeding.

"Wow, Dolly's amazing, she's done all that without a scrap of fuss."

"Nature is fantastic, isn't it?" Seth went to put a hand over hers, but she moved it away.

"Are you okay?" He gave her a quizzical look. "Have I done something to upset you?"

"It was just a conversation I had with Ben's sister. I got the feeling you're all worrying I'll be single forever."

"Is that what Daisy said?" Seth shook his head. "The only thing we talked about was how important working with children is to you. As far as I know, Ben hasn't mentioned what happened with Josh to Daisy, and I certainly haven't. She's just got a way of saying things sometimes that upset people, even when she doesn't mean to."

"I just don't want you to think I'm some sort of tragic Bridget Jones type, who cries into their pillow at night because I haven't got a boyfriend."

"I'd never think that, but does it matter even if I did?"

"I don't know, does it?"

"I'd like it to, but Ben has threatened to string me up if I do anything to upset you! And I'm off to live in America in less than a month, otherwise..." He sighed. "Ever wish you weren't in the wrong place at the wrong time?"

"Only for about five years!" She gave a brittle little laugh and he put an arm round her, as they watched Dolly and her kids settle into family life.

Chapter Seven

The children were due to start arriving at the summer camp at ten o'clock. Some of them would be staying on site with house parents or carers and others would be going home at the end of each day. All the children lived with their parents the rest of the time, rather than being in residential care, so it would be a big adjustment for those who were staying over, and some of them had never spent a night away from their parents before.

"Thank you all for coming in early." Peter Coleman addressed the summer camp staff, who'd congregated in the chapel for a first day briefing. "We've got twenty-two young people joining us for the camp with a range of disabilities, some of whom will have one-to-one carers with them at all times. I think most of the staff know each other, but if I can ask everyone just to do a thirty second introduction to their background and what your role at camp will be, I think it will help those who are new to the team this year."

Olivia listened to the introductions as they went around the room, trying to employ the same memory techniques she used as a teacher to help her remember everyone's names. She offered her own introduction and wondered if anyone would remember who she was, or if she'd have to start every sentence for the next few days by introducing herself all over again.

"I'm Seth Ramsey. I actually work in zoology as a day job, but I'm in Kelsea Bay for another month and I thought I'd see what I could do to help out." She hadn't noticed Seth slip into the back of the chapel behind where she was sitting and he was the last to introduce himself. "I've been volunteering with the Riding for the Disabled charity for a few years and so I've come to help out with riding lessons and some of the activities on the farm. I think it's a great thing the school's doing and I'm very happy to be part of it."

“Welcome everyone!” Peter clapped his hands together. “We’ve had some wonderful news, actually. I’m sure most of you will have attended the annual Sheep Grand National at Coppergate Farm run by Julian London?” Olivia had absolutely no idea what he was talking about, but everyone else seemed to be in the know and were nodding their heads enthusiastically. “For those of you who don’t know, each year the Sheep Grand National raises money from entry fees and bets on the race for a local charity. This year they’ve chosen to support the summer camp and agreed that any remaining funds can be sent to St Josephine’s, our school out in Africa. “

“What are we going to use the money for, Peter? A big thank you meal for your loyal staff at the end of the camp!” A woman with ruddy cheeks, and a body warmer that looked too small to do up, laughed as she made the suggestion.

“Grateful as I am to you for giving up some of your summer holiday, Penny, as you well know this money is for the children’s benefit. As such, we thought rather than having the usual barbeque at the end of camp, we could have a proper party with some professional entertainment and gifts for all the children as a memento of the camp. Hopefully we’ll also be buying some new stationery and equipment for the start of term at St Josephine’s.”

There was a rumble of conversation as people began to come up with ideas about what they could do for the children at the end of camp celebration. Peter let it run for a few minutes before he held up his hand.

“That’s something we can decide later, but I just wanted to let you know the good news. For now, Felicity has everyone's schedules for this first week, the children you’ll be working with and where the activities will be held. When you aren’t leading a session, we’ve pencilled you in to help out other staff, so the children get as much attention as possible in every session.”

Felicity, the head teacher's assistant, moved around the room handing out the schedules. Olivia scanned the sheet she was given and sighed with relief that she hadn't been put on the rota to help out on the farm. Seth had told her there were some free-range geese nesting on the edge of the pond and the last thing she wanted was to terrify the children by screaming if any of the birds came near her. She'd been scheduled to help Seth with his riding lessons on Thursday afternoons, but she could cope with horses even if her old riding instructor had said she'd never be a proper rider. They weren't all that different to Gerald, it was just birds she didn't trust.

****

The first day of summer camp was hectic and fun, and reminded Olivia all over again why she loved teaching children with special needs. Sometimes it was so challenging that you barely knew if you'd make it through the day. And there were the moments like the ones with Connor, on the first afternoon of summer camp, that made it all worthwhile.

"What are you making?" Olivia leant over the young boy's shoulder, as he pushed two pieces of clay together and pinched the end with his fingers to make them stick.

"I'm making my house, so I can go home. I don't want to stay here tonight." Connor turned towards her and gave her a blistering look, as if she were the person responsible for making him stay at camp.

"It'll be lots of fun. There's a big TV room and they're going to show one of the Star Wars movies tonight and I've heard there might even be hot dogs and popcorn." Olivia crouched by the side of his wheelchair, but he'd gone back to jabbing at the clay shapes in front of him, which didn't much resemble a house.

"I've seen all the Star Wars films already and I can have popcorn at home. I just want to go back and see my mum and dad, and Jasper."

"I'll tell you what, you carry on working on the house and I'll see if I can find out what else they're planning for tonight. I'm sure there'll be something going on that will make you glad you're staying over." Leaving the teaching assistant to watch Connor and another little boy, Sanjay, she went over to the desk and picked up Connor's file. There was a care plan inside with some notes on his condition and a bit of background on his home life. Connor, who was eleven, had a form of muscular dystrophy and he needed to use a wheelchair all the time. The notes explained that it was his first time away from home and that his parents were planning to spend some one-on-one time with his little brother Alex, whilst Connor was at the camp. Olivia had seen it before, parents with a child who had disabilities sometimes spent so much of their energy meeting the needs of that child, that any siblings they might have often felt overlooked. But if Connor's little brother was called Alex, then who was Jasper?

"There's going to be a games night after the film and a chance to win some iTunes vouchers for the person with the most points at the end of each week." Olivia already knew from the weekly schedule exactly what activities were going on every evening.

"I don't like music." Connor wasn't giving an inch and didn't even look at her, squashing the clay into a ball again instead.

"What would you like to do, if you had the choice of doing anything?"

"I just want to sit and watch TV with Jasper on my lap like I do at home."

"Is Jasper your dog?"

"No, I don't like dogs. Jasper's a cat. Cats are much cleverer than dogs, everyone knows that."

"I'm sure Jasper's missing you too. But you know that one of the good things about going away is that, even though you might miss people and your pets, it just makes going home even better and more exciting when you get to see them again." Olivia wasn't even sure she was convincing herself, let alone Connor, who was frowning so hard she could hardly see his eyes. She was grateful to be saved by a knock on the art room door.

"Sorry, Mr Coleman just asked me to pop in and see if there was anything I could do to help, as the last student I was due to teach decided they didn't want to go riding after all." Seth stood in the doorway, but he wasn't alone. "For heaven's sake, Hugo, stop following me, I haven't got anything else to give you!" The school's cat snaked between his legs and Connor's face was immediately transformed.

"Whose cat is that?" Connor reached down with his hand as Hugo sauntered over to him, obviously recognising a soft touch when he saw one.

"He lives on the school farm, but I made the mistake of giving him a bit of ham out of one of my sandwiches at lunch time and ever since I've had a new best friend." Seth shook his head, but it looked as if he was about to lose his place in Hugo's affections.

"Do you think Mr Coleman would let me have Hugo on my lap whilst we watch the film? It'll be almost as good as having Jasper there."

"I don't see why not." Olivia hoped she was right, it was the happiest she'd seen Connor all day.

"Can you lift him up on to my lap, please, he's a bit heavy for me?" Connor turned to Olivia with an irresistible smile. He looked like a completely different boy from the sulky pre-teen he'd been five minutes before.

"There you go, be a good boy Hugo." The cat didn't need telling twice. He settled down on Connor's lap and was soon purring loudly, a match made in heaven.

"Can Miss Middleton take me to see Mr Coleman, please? It won't be so bad staying over if I'm allowed to sit with Hugo at night?" As Connor spoke, Olivia looked over at the teaching assistant who nodded her head, both of them just pleased to see Connor finally starting to enjoy himself.

"Off you go then, but remember if Mr Coleman says no, he'll have a good reason." Connor waved his hand in response. He couldn't wait to get out of the door and Olivia very much doubted he'd be willing to listen to reason, if the head teacher didn't let him keep hold of Hugo.

"Sorry, I didn't mean to disrupt your lesson." Seth looked worn out. "I hadn't realised how demanding this would be, though, balancing the kids' emotions and trying to encourage them to do stuff they've never done before. I'm exhausted even though the day seemed to fly by. I'm not in again until Thursday, but I'll need that long to recover."

"Well, you instantly had more success with Connor and I've been doing this for nearly ten years." Olivia glanced quickly at Sanjay, who was still happily making a pot out of clay.

"I can't really take credit for that, I've been trying to shake that cat off all afternoon!"

"Things happen for a reason and I'm really glad you gave Hugo a bit of your lunch. When Connor's face lit up like it did, I'd happily have given Hugo a whole side of ham."

"Things do happen for a reason." Seth gave her one of his thoughtful looks. "Did you see that you've been scheduled to help me with the riding lessons on Thursday?"

"Yes, I had noticed that." It was hardly a huge twist of fate. Almost all the staff were helping out other team members at some point.

"I'll look forward to Thursday, then, but right now, if you don't need me for anything, I'm off home to Ben's. I've got a feeling I'll be flat out by nine o'clock, I don't remember feeling this tired for a long time."

"I'll look forward to Thursday too." Olivia smiled. "But my day's not over yet, Sanjay's still got his masterpiece to finish."

“Don’t work too hard.” He closed the door quietly and Sanjay didn’t even look up. It had been a good first day and Seth was right about the time whizzing past, although suddenly Thursday seemed a long way off.

Chapter Eight

Bad timing seemed to be a theme of Seth's time in Kelsea Bay. First there'd been the news about Daisy wanting to take her money out of the surgery and the flat, with very little notice for Ben, and then there was the kiss with Olivia. He was still trying to solve the first problem. Ben had refused his offer of an interest free loan to cover the return of Daisy's investment. Seth had sold his flat in Edinburgh in the first week of it being on the market. He hadn't wanted the hassle of renting the place out while he was in the States and it had sold so quickly he knew he'd made the right decision. Then, when he'd realised that Ben could do with a loan, it had seemed even more like it was meant to be. But Ben was determined not to borrow money from family or friends again, and so he'd gone ahead and applied for the re-mortgage of the surgery and the two-bedroom flat above it. Seth was trying to work out how he might persuade Ellie and Ben to let him invest in their plans for the farm instead, but he'd have to approach it carefully.

In some ways the kiss was a far more pleasant problem. He liked Olivia more and more and it had seemed the most natural thing in the world for them to kiss to celebrate getting through the song at the anniversary party. But it was a bit like sneaking a tiny bit of butter cream off the side of a cake that no-one would notice, the problem was you ended up wanting more. It was bad timing again. He might even risk his friendship with Ben if he made a move, and his growing friendship with Ellie would almost certainly be over. Some things weren't meant to be, so a long run in the countryside that stretched out from Kelsea Bay was the best thing to clear his head. Exercise had always helped him get his thoughts straight and maybe he'd even come up with a solution to persuade Ben to let him invest in the farm.

It was hilly around the bay and the run had been just what he'd needed, using up the excess energy he had on the days he wasn't working. He slowed down to a gentler pace as he started the final descent back into the bay, passing a piece of scrubland almost hidden behind a row of ramshackle sheds. There was a rickety wooden gate at the entrance to the land, with building rubble dumped over most of the grass. He'd never been this way before and it was a bit of an eyesore compared to everywhere else around Kelsea Bay. There was a 'sold' sign on the corner of the land and it had no doubt been snapped up for redevelopment. Seth had been about to pick up the pace again when he'd seen it - a piebald horse standing in one corner of the scrubland, its head was hanging low and it was standing awkwardly, not able to get a steady footing amongst the rubble. There was no way Seth could just leave it. He had to check the horse was okay. Not wanting to risk opening the gate in case it fell apart altogether, he managed to take a run up and jump over it, nearly falling on the other side as his feet landed on the rubble. This was no place to keep an animal and the horse didn't even react when he walked towards it.

"You okay, boy?" As he got closer, he could see the horse was male and the animal was in an even worse condition than he'd feared. The head collar he was wearing had obviously been cutting into his head for some time and his ribs were visibly sticking out even through his unclipped coat. He eventually moved his head and gave Seth a mournful look, too listless to actually move, even if Seth presented a threat.

"What the hell do you think you're doing?" A shout from behind made Seth turn quickly, and he nearly lost his footing again on the rough ground. "This is private property and I could have you arrested for trespassing. If you're one of those bloody surveyors again, measuring up for what the new owners are going to put here, you can get lost. They don't officially own it until next week and I might still pull out if they keep sending idiots like you 'round here." The man was probably only middle-aged, but he looked as if he'd had a rough life. His face was bright red with indignation and, every time he opened his mouth to shout at Seth again, it was clear it had been a very long time since he'd seen a dentist.

"I'm not from any surveying firm, but if we're talking about arrests, I'm the one who should be having you arrested for keeping an animal in these conditions." Seth suspected his own face had gone quite red, he hadn't been this angry for a long time.

"Oh you're one of *those*! I suppose you care more about animals than people, don't you?"

"Definitely more than *some* people."

"Where were you when they told me I couldn't live in one of my sheds anymore? I wasn't bothering anyone, but it brings down the tone of the neighbourhood they said. That's all people around here care about - the value of their bloody houses and roaring up these lanes in their overpriced cars, polluting the atmosphere with chemicals." The man shook his head and his fist at the same time. "Me and Joey were quite happy here until all this."

"If Joey's the horse's name, he looks anything but happy to me." Seth clenched his fists to his sides. He'd never been in a fight but he could happily have swung for the man who'd inflicted so much pain on Joey. The head collar had rubbed away patches of hair all over the horse's head and the skin underneath was raw and bleeding, his hooves were overgrown and his flanks hollow. He was in a very sorry state, and frankly Seth couldn't have cared less if the man's shed was bulldozed with him inside it.

"He'll be out of his misery soon, so there's no point in reporting me. The knacker's yard have offered me thirty quid for him." The man narrowed his eyes, daring Seth to object. "You're to blame, you nosy sod, you and all the others like you.

Poking your nose in where it isn't needed and messing up my life, forcing me to stop living like I was, and now I've had no choice but to sell the land. I've got nowhere to keep Joey now, even if I wanted to."

"Sell him to me instead."

"I wouldn't sell him to you for three times the price they've offered me."

"What about ten times the price?" As Seth asked the question the man's face changed. Greed over-taking his indignation.

"You'd pay three hundred quid for that mangy bag of bones? All he's good for is dog food but, if you've got more money than sense, then far be it from me to stop you. A fool and his money have always been easily parted."

"If you come down to Kelsea Bay with me now, I'll get the money out of the cashpoint and we can come back and I'll take Joey straight away. Otherwise the deal's off." Seth held his breath, hoping his bluff would pay off and thanking the habit he had of keeping a bank card in the back pocket of his running shorts, just in case he needed it unexpectedly. He'd always thought it was more likely that he'd use it to pay for a taxi home if he got injured out running, he'd never once imagined that it would result in him coming home with a horse in tow. But he didn't trust Joey's owner to keep to the deal otherwise. He might just be vindictive enough to have disappeared by the time Seth got back and end up sticking with his original plan for Joey.

"Whatever." The man grumbled, but he grudgingly turned towards the gate and Seth followed him. "But if you think I'm jogging down there after you, you've got another think coming."

****

"How much did you pay for him?" Ben finished looking inside Joey's mouth and turned to Seth.

"Three hundred pounds."

"I'd say they saw you coming, but I think he'd have been dead within a week if you hadn't stepped in, even without a trip to the slaughterhouse."

"Is he going to be alright?" Olivia looked close to tears as she stood with Ellie, watching Ben and Seth checking the horse over.

"I think so. We'll need to treat his wounds and get a farrier up to sort his feet out as soon as possible, and feed him up of course." Ben shook his head, still looking as if he was struggling to take in how Joey had been treated. "But he can only be about six or seven. So if he's got the will to survive, he should be able to make it through. I've already spoken to one of my friends who works for the RSPCA and he wants us to take some photographs, so that they can pursue a case against Joey's old owner, to make sure he's banned from keeping animals again."

"That's great. And you're sure you don't mind keeping him here, Ellie?" Seth looked across at Ben's fiancée, who was nodding her head.

"Absolutely. It's the least we can do for him."

"I'm going to pay the going rate for livery though, I don't care what you say."

"We'll talk about that later, let's just concentrate on getting Joey well first." Whatever Ellie said, Seth was determined to pay for Joey to stay at the farm. Maybe paying top whack livery fees would help a tiny bit, even if just covered the cost of the feed for some of the other animals Ellie had taken in. He just wished he could do more. Neither Ellie or Ben had hesitated when he'd asked them to help with Joey, and Olivia hadn't left the horse's side either since she'd got home from work.

"He's quite a handsome chap isn't he? Underneath all that missing fur." Olivia's voice caught on the words and Seth could see how much Joey had got to her too. "I hadn't realised until just now that he's got one blue eye and one brown eye."

"They call it a wall eye, but I think it gives him extra character, like David Bowie." Ben spoke as he lifted up one of Joey's hooves.

"Joey Bowie, that's got quite ring to it." Seth laughed as the horse finally lifted his head in response, he clearly approved of his new name too. "That settles it then, I think he's found a new home and a new name all in one afternoon."

"It's good to know that there are still some good guys around. You and Ben are slowly restoring my faith in men." Olivia looked at him for slightly longer than necessary and he felt that pull towards her again, before shrugging it off. It was never going to happen.

"We do our best, but Joey's the real star hanging on through everything." Seth touched her arm briefly, as he moved past her to go and phone the farrier. If he hesitated he might not be able to stop himself asking her to go for a drink with him, to celebrate Joey's second chance at life on Channel View Farm. Staying in the friend zone was for the best, he just had to keep reminding himself of that.

Chapter Nine

"What are you doing with your day off?" Ellie was brushing Ginger outside the back door of the farmhouse, the little dog desperate to escape her makeover.

"I don't consider it a day off, it's a farm work day. So, the real question is, what do you want me to do?" It was already past nine a.m. and Olivia felt guilty for having had her first lie in since she'd arrived at Channel View Farm. After two days working flat out at the summer camp, even the sound of Gerald braying and the cockerel desperately trying to out-do him, hadn't been enough to wake her up.

"This is going to sound weird." Ellie let go of Ginger, who shot out of arm's reach and immediately started rolling on the grass, trying to undo all of Ellie's good work.

"I've got used to doing unusual jobs around here and it can't be any worse than having to sing at a party."

"Well I think I can beat that, because today's job is sheep training." Ellie was laughing so much she could hardly get the words out. "See I told you it was weird."

"Okay, you've got me."

"You've heard about the Sheep Grand National, right?"

"Yes, they're donating all the proceeds to the school. But if you saw the list of things the staff have suggested the money is used for, even the proceeds from the real Grand National wouldn't cover it!"

"It's a great cause and we want to do our part." Ellie pulled a face. "Although I've got to be honest, there is an ulterior motive. We're going to race a couple of our sheep and Mum has made them little cloth saddles that advertise the farm, and she's also going to make a load of cakes for after the race. We thought it might be a way of getting our name out there and reminding people what we do up here."

"Well it's certainly different from an ad in the local paper."

"The diary is looking worryingly empty after the last of the wedding bookings in September. I wasn't too bothered at first, but the months are racing by now and the bills won't stop just because wedding season does." Ellie shrugged, but her words were anything but casual.

"I've told you, I've got quite a bit saved up, and I'm more than happy to help out to get you through a sticky patch if you need it."

"I love you, Liv, but I couldn't take your money in a million years." Ellie forced a smile. "Anyway, Alan has already offered to bail me out and Ben is going to put some money into the farm, but none of it is a long-term solution. We were thinking of applying for planning permission to open a soft play centre, but Ben has already had to re-mortgage the flat, to pay someone back the money they lent him when he became a partner in the surgery; so he can't put in as much money as he'd originally planned to. It's reminded me that I can't rely on other people's generosity, not even from my oldest friend. We're thinking about borrowing the money for the soft-play centre, but Mum's got all her money from the sale of the old house tied up in this place and I can't risk having too much of a debt against that. And now it looks like the roof on the farmhouse is going to need replacing at some point. If the farm's going to work as a venue long term, we've got to become known for more than just weddings and anniversary parties. But it's okay because world domination will start with a victory at the Sheep Grand National."

"I just want you to remember that the offer's there, if you need it."

"Thanks, Liv, but the subject's closed. We've got sheep training to concentrate on."

"How are we going to train the sheep? Don't we need a dog to do that? Somehow I don't think Ginger is going to be up to it." Accepting the change of subject she looked at the dog, who had now found a patch of dust to lie in, sunbathing with her belly exposed and her front paws bent over like a meerkat.

"We probably could use a dog if mine wasn't more interested in sleeping than anything else! I inherited Holly, one of the sheep I want to enter, from Julian who hosts the race at his farm. She's got a bit of a limp and was going to be slaughtered if we didn't rehome her, as Julian didn't think she'd be up to having lambs. So his little girl, Maisie, begged me to take Holly. I wanted Holly and Betsy, the other sheep we're entering, to have a few practice runs first so they don't get injured."

"In case it ends their racing career?" If someone had told Olivia six months before that she'd be training for a Sheep Grand National, she'd have laughed even harder than she was now.

"All we've got to do is put them on a lead rope and run about a hundred metres with them."

"Never mind the sheep needing training, I could have done with some warning myself!" Running had never been Olivia's thing, and then there was that sports day at secondary school when she'd tripped and gone sprawling into Rob Bennett, a good looking sixth former who almost everyone had a crush on. She'd been able to hear him and his friends laughing all the way back to the changing rooms. But she was a grown up now; if she fell over and was trampled by a herd of sheep with white line fever, as long as it raised plenty of money, it was all worthwhile.

****

By the time they got down to the bottom paddock, with the two sheep reluctantly following them, when there was so much lush green grass to stop and enjoy on the way, Karen and Alan were already waiting for them. Alan had roped out two lanes for the sheep to race in and Karen was waiting at the finishing line with her iPhone held out in front of her.

"You're not going to video us, are you?" Olivia pulled at the bottom of her tee-shirt, wondering if it was too late to go back to the farm and put a coat on, despite the heat.

"It's for the website and Alan is learning how to use Twitter, we thought we could put it on there to advertise the race and Channel View Farm. It might help people realise there's more to us than just the wedding photos we've got on the website at the moment." Karen was looking so cheerful that Olivia didn't have the heart to put a dampener on her idea, even though the thought of being videoed running, and probably failing to keep up with the sheep she was supposed to be training, made her want to run even faster in the opposite direction.

"I'm going to time you, to see whether we've got a chance of winning." Alan wasn't joking, he'd moved next to Karen on the finishing line with a stopwatch in his hand. Was this really what people in the country did to pass the time?

"So have we got a speed we're aiming for?" She decided she might as well enter into the spirit of things, but she had no idea how fast sheep were supposed to be able to run.

"No idea really." Alan shrugged, a twinkle in his eye that suggested he wasn't taking this quite so seriously after all. "But at least we can work out if Holly and Betsy are getting any quicker."

"Shall we put a wager on it, to make it more interesting? Whoever gets the fastest time today gets to choose a forfeit for the other?" Ellie grinned and Olivia had a horrible feeling she knew what her forfeit was going to be.

"Okay, but why do I think I'm going to regret this?"

"Because I'm going to make you open up the chicken hutch every morning. You know facing your fears is the best way to get over them."

"Well, in that case," Olivia laughed, "you know what I'm going to make you do if I win, don't you?"

"No, you wouldn't!" Ellie shook her head.

"There must be a circus on somewhere nearby, think of all those lovely clowns, just waiting to help you get over your phobia."

"Don't! It makes me shiver just thinking about it."

"Well you better be the Usain Bolt of the sheep racing world then." Olivia didn't miss the determined look on Ellie's face as she spoke.

"You'll be eating mine and Betsy's dust!" As soon as Alan shouted 'go', Ellie was true to her word, running down the paddock with Betsy trotting after her. Holly wasn't quite so keen and there was no rushing her, despite all the clicking and whistling Olivia tried. Three races down, and Ellie and Betsy had stormed all of them, but Olivia felt like a winner anyway. She hadn't laughed that much in months, years probably. It was like being a child all over again, doing things just for the sheer fun of them. Something that had always been easier with Ellie than with any other friend she'd ever had.

"How's Joey doing? I haven't had much time to go and see him these last couple of days, but last time I checked in on him he seemed to be making up for lost time with his eating." Olivia sat on the grass next to her best friend, watching the two sheep grazing, all of them taking a well-deserved rest.

"Ben said he's doing really well and whenever Seth turns up, Joey follows him around like a lap dog." Ellie laughed. "I think he knows he owes his life to Seth and, when he's had a couple more weeks to recover from the worst of his injuries, I'm going to put him in the field with Gerald."

"That's such great news and you're brilliant with all the animals that no-one else seems to want. But why do I get the feeling you knew exactly what you were doing when you chose to race Betsy?"

"What me?" Ellie tried and failed to look surprised. "You know it was never really about winning the race, don't you? We just wanted you to have some fun. You've worked flat out almost since your plane landed and I can't thank you enough for your help last weekend."

"There's no need to thank me and I was already having fun, even if it doesn't always look like it." She squeezed Ellie's hand, not needing to explain that she wouldn't instantly feel like her old self, even though she was sure she'd done the right thing. "I wish there was something more I could do to help out with getting the business where it needs to be."

"Oh, don't listen to me, I'm probably panicking over nothing. It's going in the right direction, but with an old house and setting up a new business, I guess we're only ever a bad month or two away from getting into trouble. Especially if something big happens like the problems with the roof, the boiler needing replacing or one of the animals getting really sick." Ellie wrinkled her nose. "Why else do you think I'm marrying the local vet!"

"Because you're made for each other."

"It's a good job Seth can't hear you talking like that, he'd think you've gone as sentimental as me and Ben."

"Well, since he freely admits he's never been in love, he's not really in a position to judge." Olivia picked a dandelion clock and twirled the stem between her fingers, watching the seeds fly off onto the light summer breeze.

"I didn't realise the two of you had been having those sorts of deep and meaningful conversations?" Ellie took off her sunglasses and gave Olivia an intense look.

"We haven't, but when we helped out Bert and Hetty with their little dog, we got to talking about what it must be like to be married for fifty odd years like them. He said it was something he couldn't really imagine, because he hasn't had a really serious relationship."

"And what about you, is it something you can imagine yet? I know I promised not to mention it again, but since you brought it up..."

"It's not my priority for now." Olivia felt the sun on her face and a wave of pure contentment swept over her. She really didn't feel like anything was missing now she was home. Maybe being so far away from everyone she loved had made Josh's betrayal feel much worse than it really was. If it had happened in the UK, she'd have moved on with her life much sooner.

"Don't let him stop you finding someone who really deserves you, Liv. I'd hate Josh to have that sort of impact on your life."

"Now you sound just like Seth." She laughed and leant her head against Ellie's for a moment. "Don't worry, one of these days you'll get to wear a peach taffeta bridesmaid dress, just like I always promised!" Back when they were children, huddled together in their den making plans and dreaming, they'd cut pictures out of a bridal magazine someone had given them, deciding who would wear what on their big days. Olivia had chosen a pale orange bridesmaid dress for Ellie, which much like dinners at Pizza Hut, had seemed the height of sophistication at the time.

"I'll hold you to that." Ellie squeezed her hand again. "You know that this has been my best wedding present, don't you? Just having you home."

"Does that mean you're going to let me off sorting out the chickens every morning?"

"Not on your life." Ellie jumped to her feet. "In fact, I was thinking of getting some geese."

Olivia threw a handful of grass in her direction. "You can go off people you know!"

****

It was such a beautiful afternoon on Thursday that Olivia was glad to escape from the classroom, even if she was nervous about being more of hindrance than a help to Seth with his riding lessons. Pulling on her wellies, despite the warm weather, she headed over to the sand ménage where the riding lessons were held. Large letters were printed on signs positioned on fence posts around the sand school, so that Seth could instruct the children and their helpers which way to go with the ponies to criss-cross the ménage and learn to improve their control of the ponies.

"Okay Libby, just try and relax a little bit, push your heels down into the stirrups if you can and hold on to the neck strap if you want to. I think we're ready for a trot." Seth was running alongside the pony, whilst the learning support assistant held on to Libby's leg to keep her steady. The little girl went from a wide-eyed look of terror when the pony first started to trot, to giggling as she bounced up and down and settled into some sort of rhythm. Seth was encouraging her all the way and when she dismounted, it was obvious that Libby wasn't used to that sort of movement. Although walking was clearly difficult, she threw her arms first around Seth and then the pony.

"That was the best day ever!"

"You did so well, Libby." Seth gave her the thumbs up.

"Can I ride Barney again, please?"

"Absolutely. Same time next week?"

"Okay, but can I come down and see Barney in between?" Libby gave him another one of her killer smiles. "I could give him some of my carrots, because I don't really like them anyway."

"I'm sure you can come down and see him lots. I'll ask Mr Coleman if someone can bring you down tomorrow, but it might be best if you eat the carrots as they can make ponies fat if they eat too many. But for girls your age, they're perfect for building up your strength and can help you get really good at riding."

"Really?"

"Absolutely." Libby finally seemed satisfied and after another over enthusiastic hug of the long-suffering pony, she held on to the fence to take the ten or so steps she needed to leave the ménage, so that the learning support assistant could help her back into her wheelchair.

"You certainly seem to have a way of bringing children and animals together." Olivia walked into the ménage, as Libby disappeared around the corner with the learning support assistant having to jog to keep up with her electric wheelchair.

"Libby's a fantastic kid, she's got cerebral palsy, but she worked really hard today and had a go at everything I asked her to do, even when I could tell she was scared. Barney is brilliant though and he seems to sense when the children need him to be extra steady, he's the perfect pony for this job. Sometimes I almost wish I'd chosen to do something like this. I've always had a passion for zoology, but I'd forgotten how rewarding it can be to see the connection between a child and an animal and the difference it can make to them both. There's something magical about it."

"I think that's why Ellie and I loved going to stay with her Aunt Hilary so much when we were kids. There was just so much freedom and every day on the farm felt like an adventure."

"It's a great place. I don't think Joey can believe his luck that he's there, after where he was living. Ellie said she took him for a walk around the farm last night. He's not quite ready to be put out with the donkeys yet, but she said his ears were pricked up the whole time and she had a bit of trouble keeping hold of him. He's getting so strong, so quickly."

"You seem to love it here too."

"I do and if the research work ever dries up, I definitely know what my Plan B is going to be."

"Somehow I doubt that it will and I'm guessing, as much as you're enjoying it here now, it would all feel pretty tame in comparison coming back here after San Diego. How long do you think you'll be out in the States for?"

"The postings are for a year at a time and they're recruiting zoologists on sabbatical from all over the world, but there's always the opportunity of applying for a permanent post out there, which is why I resigned from my role at Edinburgh zoo. The conservation research they're doing in San Diego is ground breaking and I wanted to have the freedom to stay on if they want me to. Although I'd have to think about what happens to Joey if I do. It wouldn't be fair for me to ask Ellie to keep him forever, but I suppose there's always the option of taking him out there if I settle permanently."

"It sounds like your dream job."

"It's what I've been working towards ever since I was at university."

"I don't know what I want to do now. Other than teach, that is." Olivia shrugged. "I used to think I wanted to head up my own school, but I don't think I could stand all the admin that goes with it. It's being with the kids that I love."

"Then you've already got your dream job." Seth smiled at her, as another learning support assistant headed towards them, with the young boy who Olivia would be supporting for the next riding lesson.

"I suppose so." She nodded, but she couldn't put her finger on the empty feeling that had settled in her stomach. If teaching was really enough, then why did Seth talking about fulfilling his dreams leave her feeling so uneasy?

Chapter Ten

If the weather had been on their side for the three weeks since Olivia had come home, then the Sunday of the joint hen and stag party bucked the trend in spectacular style. Ellie and Olivia had been run off their feet the day before with a big wedding, but for once it wasn't the sound of Gerald's now familiar early morning braying that woke Olivia up, but the rain lashing against the window.

"I hope you've got a sowester and some waders ready for today?" Karen looked up from the table, where she was cutting up a loaf of bread, and smiled.

"I know! Of all the days for the weather to take a turn, it has to be the one when I've booked to take us all out on the water."

"I'm sure we'll have a wonderful time and it'll make it more memorable, the weather being like this." That was one of the things she loved about Karen, she was always so upbeat, even when things didn't turn out as planned. If there was a silver lining to be found, Karen would find it. It made Olivia homesick, in a strange sort of way, to see her own parents. She'd give her mum a ring next week and see if things were settled enough with their foster placements for Olivia to pay a visit.

"You're right and I know Ellie will make the best of it, whatever happens. I was planning to make her breakfast with some buck's fizz, so we could at least start the day off like I intended."

"Beat you to it!" Karen smiled again. "That's why I came over this morning, I thought I could make us all a nice breakfast before we head off. Alan's gone down to the bay to pick Ben and Seth up, so it's all in hand."

"What about the animals?"

"Alan was up at five to get them all sorted."

"He really is lovely that husband of yours, isn't he?"

"I'm very lucky." Karen stopped what she was doing and looked at Olivia. "But stick around Channel View Farm and I can guarantee it will be your turn next. I don't know what it is about this place, but it has a way of changing lives."

"I'm already happier than I've been for a long time."

"I'm glad to hear it, love, I really am and we're all so happy to have you home. Now off you go and get yourself ready, you've done all the hard work organising this and you've helped out so much since you got here, so I want you to have a relaxing day too."

"Thank you." Squeezing Karen's hand, there was nothing else she could say and no way she could ever repay the friendship that Ellie and Karen had shown her over the years, even if she waitressed at a thousand weddings or literally sang for her supper every night.

****

"Do you think this boat is sturdy enough to take my weight?" Karen was gripping on to Alan's arm as if her life depended on it, as she stepped into the rib, a large motorised rubber dingy that was taking them out to see the seals.

"Don't be daft of course it will." Alan shook his head, but stayed rock steady despite the boat listing to and fro as more people started to come on board. Each of the dinghies seated twelve people and Olivia had booked two of them. Along with the six of them, Ben had invited six of his other friends, as well as his partner from the veterinary practice and his wife, there were several of Ellie's friends from Kelsea Bay and a couple of the regular staff from Channel View Farm, who had become friends of both Ellie and Ben since they'd started the business. They'd also invited Caroline and Julian who owned Coppergate farm, where the Sheep Grand National was going to held. Ellie hadn't wanted to invite anyone along from her old job, or her old life before she'd moved to the farm. A couple of her friends from university were going to the wedding, but for the most part her new life in Kelsea Bay had been a fresh start for Ellie and new friendships had quickly formed – something Olivia had never allowed herself to experience in Brisbane. But she knew now that it could be done, whether she ended up staying in Kent or moving nearer to her parents in Yorkshire.

"Thanks for organising this, Liv, it was a brilliant idea." Ellie attempted to give her a hug, but the bulky lifejackets made it more of a tussle as the boat swayed a little bit more.

"It's a long time since I've had to tell you two off for messing about, but this boat is making me nervous!" Karen wagged a finger in their direction, but she was still smiling, despite keeping her other hand firmly clamped onto one of the handles on the side of the boat as it moved out of the harbour and into the open sea.

"Much as I'd like to take credit for the idea, it was all down to Bert's suggestion." It seemed like half a lifetime ago, rather than a matter of weeks. Had she only known Seth that long? Working together at the school and helping out with events at Channel View Farm had thrown them together and she already classed him as a friend.

"I'm so glad you didn't go for something obvious, like paintballing. This just feels like us."

"That's why we chose it." Olivia's words were lost in the wind as the boat picked up speed and began bouncing up and down on the waves, making everyone follow Karen's lead and grip tightly to the handles of the boat.

When the rib had been going for about fifteen minutes, it slowed down to a steadier pace and Olivia was finally able to let go of the handle that had left an imprint in her palm. Exciting as it was, she hadn't fancied getting deposited into the cold depths of the English Channel. Karen on the other hand had completely settled into the experience and had a huge grin on her face, even if her hair did look like she been plugged into the electricity for the last fifteen minutes. It was great to see her so carefree, with Alan's arm slung around her shoulders. Olivia's mum, Janet, and Karen had been friends too and she'd often overheard her parents talking about Karen when she was growing up. It had been obvious that they'd admired her for putting Ellie at the absolute centre of her world as a single parent. It was another reason Olivia couldn't wait to go to Yorkshire, so she could tell her parents just how well things had worked out for Karen.

"We're slowing down now as we approach the nature reserve." The skipper of the boat turned to speak to them. There was no microphone, so he shouted instead, making Olivia jump and grab hold of the handle on the side of the rib again. "We choose our departure times based on tidal flows to give you the best chance of seeing as many seals as possible. But the good news is that seals are just one type of wildlife you might see in the reserve. It's an absolute haven for birds and so you're guaranteed to see a wide array of them today, including egrets and herons."

"Herons are those huge ones, right?" Olivia turned to Ellie who was already laughing.

"Don't worry, Liv, we won't let them attack you." Ben who was sitting on the other side of Ellie gave her a reassuring smile. It seemed everyone knew about her bird phobia.

"We'll protect you, although they'll probably be even more scared of you than you are of them." Seth stood up, moving across to the space on the other side of Olivia, between her and Karen, as the boat slowed to a slow chug and drew level with the other rib.

"I'm not quite sure how to take that, but I think it's reassuring." Olivia moved slightly so that Seth had a bit more space, although she quite liked the solid presence of his leg against hers. He certainly looked as if he could fend off a heron should the need arise. "Anyway, it's about time I got over this bird phobia, so I'll do my best not to be a wimp about it."

"I don't think anyone could accuse you of that."

"I could always sing to them if it comes to it. That should drive them away." Despite the joke, it had surprised her just how much she'd enjoyed singing again and she couldn't remember when or why she'd stopped doing things just for the fun of it. Shortly after she'd landed in Brisbane, probably. But it was time to put that right. There was a flyer on the parish council's noticeboard in Kelsea Bay about someone starting a rock choir. If she managed to get a permanent job nearby, she'd decided to sign up.

"I told you before, you've got a great voice, I could have listened to you all night." Seth held her gaze for a moment and she knew he meant it.

"Hardly great, but I'm going to be inflicting it on the local rock choir, if I can persuade Peter Coleman to give me a job at the end of the summer camp."

"I think it's guaranteed. You're brilliant with the kids and Peter's smart enough to know when he sees someone special."

"Are you just being nice to me, to keep my mind off rampaging herons attacking the boat and bursting a hole in the side of the rib with their evil, pointy beaks?"

"Maybe." He laughed, putting a warm hand over hers. It didn't mean anything, but it felt good all the same.

"Look, I can see a seal!" Ellie jumped out of her seat and pointed over to a craggy outcrop of rocks just to the left of the boat.

"Sit down, please, or you'll be swimming over there to meet the seals in person!" The rib skipper shot Ellie a warning look and she did as she was told, but even the telling off did nothing to dampen her excitement.

"There are lots of them, they're just well camouflaged against the rocks when you first see them." The two boats moved closer to the rocks as Ellie spoke and Olivia could see several of the seals lying down, soaking up the sunshine that was finally seeing off the rain.

Everyone on board seemed to have brought a camera or a mobile phone with them and, for the next twenty minutes or so, as the ribs moved slowly through the nature reserve and looped back round, the seals were photographed so many times they could have given Kim Kardashian a run for her money.

"Does that seal look injured to you?" Olivia pointed to one of the seals, who was moving across the rocks in an even more awkward lopsided way than the rest of them did.

"He looks pretty well fed and that's usually the best sign. A healthy seal should look thick all the way down, like a slug only a lot prettier." Seth laughed. "It's when they have a neck like a dog that you need to worry, it usually means they aren't able to feed themselves properly for some reason. He's just not a great mover and, if you ever saw me dancing, you'd probably think the same thing about me!"

"I'll look forward to seeing that at the wedding then!"

The ribs picked up speed again, as they headed back towards Kelsea Bay, where they'd organised a meal in the deli and bistro Daisy ran with Ben's mum. It would be a chance to relax after their morning of excitement and no doubt give Daisy the chance to take centre stage. Although, when she'd spoken to Olivia earlier in the week, it was clear she was pulling out all the stops for Ben and Ellie, so her suspicion that Daisy's heart was in the right place was proving true.

The weather started to change again as they got closer to Kelsea Bay. It was still much sunnier than it had been when they'd left, but the wind seemed to have picked up.

"Oh God, is that someone in the water up ahead?" Karen shouted out, at the same time as the boat skipper spotted the person in the water in front of them. Turning the boat in a sharp circle, he cut the engines, as the other rib flew past them still heading towards the beach.

"Are you okay?" The skipper shouted to the boy in the water, who Olivia could now see clearly. He looked to be in his late teens, his eyes wide in an otherwise expressionless face.

"I am, but my girlfriend..." The boy shook his head, as the boat inched nearer and Ben and Seth reached over the side to pull him in.

"What happened?" Ben spoke to the boy who was shivering so much he couldn't get his words out and Seth took his jacket off and laid it over the boy, along with the blanket that had been draped across Karen's knees.

"Sh, sh, she..." His teeth were still chattering. Heaven knows how long he'd been in the water and, this far out, the recent sunshine had done nothing to warm it up. "Carly was on an inflatable rubber ring and I had hold of her, I swam out a bit and promised I wouldn't let go. Only the wind took the ring and I told her to jump off but she wouldn't. Carly's not a strong swimmer and she was scared of letting go. I tried to swim after it, but she drifted out that way, towards the buoy." He pointed ahead and to the left, his hands shaking even more than his voice.

"Can we go after her?" Seth asked and the rib skipper nodded in response.

"I'm just going to radio the other rib and ask them to call the coastguard in case they need to scramble the helicopter, but we'll see if we can find her in the meantime." He turned and looked around at the passengers. "I take it everyone's okay with that?"

"Of course we are, let's get moving, there's a young girl out there stranded in the water." Alan spoke for everyone and there was a murmur of agreement, as the skipper radioed through to the other rib and then started the engine again.

"What's your name?" Seth shouted to the boy, whose eyes were filling up with tears which had nothing to do with the wind whipping at their faces as they sped towards the buoy.

"Jack."

"Okay, Jack, were going to get to Carly, but we've got to try and warm you up to stop you getting hyperthermia. I know you don't feel like eating right now, but it's important that you have something to give you the energy your body needs to get your temperature back up where it should be." Seth handed the boy a bar of chocolate and Olivia rummaged under her seat.

"I've still got the flask of tea Karen made us all, that might help too." She handed it to Seth, who poured some into a travel mug with a lid that Jack could drink out of, even with the boat bouncing across the water. Seth didn't seem to notice the hot tea spilling over his hands as he tipped it from the flask into the mug.

"I can see her!" It was the second time Ellie had jumped up, but this time no-one was going to shout at her to sit down. As the rib slowed down again, Olivia spotted Carly, still holding on to the rubber ring with one hand and the edge of the buoy with the other. As they got closer still, it was obvious how cold she was, her lips tinged with blue. She must have been in the water for a long time and, if she'd been clinging on like that and not moving, the cold would have affected her even more.

"You need to let go, Carly, so we can get you into the boat." Ben spoke as the rib skipper lined one side of the boat up with where Carly was wedged between the buoy and the oversized rubber ring that had carried her out to it. It wasn't possible to reach out and pull her in, unless she let go of the buoy first. Carly shook her head, looking even more terrified than Jack had five minutes before.

"Please, Carls, just let go. They'll pull you in like they did me." Jack reached out his arm, which was still shaking, but Carly just shook her head again and started to sob. Maybe it was the crying, or the fact that a seagull swooped low over the boat, but something in Olivia seemed to take over and she let go of the handle she'd been holding tightly when the rib had sped towards the buoy. Standing up, she swung her legs over the side of the rib, and plunged into the water. The cold was a shock, as her head dipped below the surface, but she began swimming round the side of the boat as everyone on board started shouting. She heard a splash behind her and realised Seth was in the water too.

"What on earth do you think you're doing? I was going to get in and so was Ben." He was obviously a faster swimmer than her and he caught up with her as she rounded the boat, about ten strokes away from the buoy.

"I couldn't just sit there and do nothing." This wasn't the time to get into a debate about why it was a much better idea for Seth or Ben to have jumped in, especially when it was painfully obvious that he was a much stronger swimmer than her.

As she got to the buoy, Olivia grabbed onto it too. Silently praying that this wasn't going to turn into one of those situations where an amateur rescuer just makes the situation worse and ends up giving the professionals – or in this case Seth – two casualties to rescue instead of one.

"Come on Carly, you've got to let go, you can hold onto my shoulders and I'll swim us back to the boat." Seth's voice was calm, but he must have been as worried as Olivia.

"I can't do it. I'm not a good swimmer and you might let go of me, like Jack did." Carly's words were barely a whisper but she was still shaking her head.

"Listen, if I can make it from the boat to here, then anyone can." Olivia manoeuvred herself around the buoy so that Carly could see her face. "I'm such a chicken that I only jumped into the water to get out of the way of a seagull. And I promise you that Seth won't let you go, you can definitely rely on him."

Carly looked at her for what felt like an eternity, before whispering again. "Promise?"

"I promise."

Slowly unfurling her hands from the side of the buoy, Carly gripped Seth's shoulders so tightly that her fingers went white. He moved steadily towards the boat with Olivia following on behind. Ben, Alan and a couple of the other lads hauled all three of them on to the boat, wrapping Carly in coats and a first aid blanket, while Olivia and Seth made do with a couple of old towels that had been lying at the front of the boat.

"I'm sorry I shouted, but you scared the life out of me jumping into the water like that, before I even had the chance to react." Seth leant against her, having to half-shout into her ear as the rib sped back towards the harbour.

"I should just have left it to you."

"She wouldn't have let go of the buoy if you hadn't been there to convince her."

"We make quite a double act, don't we?" She tried to smile, even though the cold seemed to be seeping deeper into her bones with every wave the rib hit.

"We do." Seth's lips brushed against hers. "I'm sorry about that too, but I'm just so glad you're okay."

"You too." There was so much more Olivia could have said, but taking a risk on a summer romance felt like asking for trouble. After wasting so much time, she knew she should be grabbing life with both hands, and seeing how differently things could have ended for Carly and Jack seemed all the more reason to make the most of every second. But by the time the rib slowed down enough to talk normally again the moment had passed, which was probably just as well.

****

"I'd like to raise a toast to my brother, Benji, and my lovely soon-to-be sister-in-law, Ellie!" Daisy lifted her glass in the air from her position at the top of the table. Even though she was doing her best to make the afternoon in the bistro all about Ben and Ellie, she had a way of twisting things back around to her. Ben was *her* brother, and Ellie was *her* sister-in-law to be, rather than the bride-to-be, that would unmistakably make her the centre of attention. Daisy was also wearing an over-sized tee-shirt with the words *'baby on board'* emblazoned across the front, as if anyone could miss that she was pregnant.

"Thank you, Daisy, and thanks so much to you and Mum for laying on this amazing spread for us this afternoon." Ben stood to raise a toast of his own. "We've had a brilliant day so far, although there's perhaps been a bit more excitement than we originally planned!"

"Oh, let's not start talking about Olivia and Seth's heroics again!" Daisy all but heckled her brother and the look on her face suggested she wasn't joking. "We've already had to delay the start of the meal while they went home to get changed. And I'm not even sure we should be calling it heroics; a lot of people might call it stupid."

"But none of those people are here, are they Daze?" Ben looking pointedly as his sister, who reluctantly shook her head. "As I was saying, we've had a bit more excitement than originally planned but I'm delighted to say that I've had a text from Jack to say that both he and Carly have been checked out at the hospital, and they've both been cleared to go home."

"That's great news!" Seth lifted his glass. "To Carly and Jack and a lucky escape."

"Absolutely." Ben raised his glass and everyone around the table joined in, even Daisy. "But I have a couple of other toasts I want to make too. I've already thanked Daisy, Mum and their team, but this day wouldn't have been possible without two other people Ellie and I feel so lucky to be able to call our best friends. Deep sea rescues aside, I'd like us all to raise a glass to Seth and Liv, a perfect team if ever there was one."

“To Seth and Liv!” Everyone around Olivia held up their glasses but she kept her focus on Ben. She didn’t want to see if Daisy had opted out of toasting her, but it was almost as if she could feel her eyes boring into the back of her neck. She wasn’t sure what she’d said or done to upset Ben’s sister, or if was just the fact that the rescue meant people were less interested in what Daisy had to say, but it was awkward all the same.

“Thank you all for coming today and helping us to kick the wedding celebrations off early, and not minding too much that you haven’t had the chance to chain me naked to a lamppost and shave off my eyebrows.” Ben laughed and looked straight in his friend Julian’s direction. “I’ll say a lot more about this at the wedding of course, so you better get yourselves ready for it, but I couldn’t finish the toasts today without talking about my beautiful fiancée, Ellie. I know some of you think it’s odd that we chose to spend our stag and hen day together, but there’s never anywhere else I’d rather be than with her. To Ellie and counting down the days until I can call her my wife.”

“To Ellie.” Olivia raised her glass to her best friend, locking eyes with Seth across the table from her. Did he still think Ben and Ellie’s declarations of love were toe-curling? She couldn’t pretend any longer, that seeing two such perfectly matched people together didn’t make her a little bit wistful for what she might never have. Rubbing her eyes with the back of her hand, she took another sip of champagne. Realising for the first time that to *really* love someone it had to be a two-way thing. That person had to be prepared to give things up to be with you and not even see them as a sacrifice, exactly the way Ben and Ellie did. Maybe she’d never really been in love with Josh. After all, how could you love someone, when you’d never really known them at all?

****

Seth felt as though every bone in his body ached by the time he got back to the flat after the hen and stag day. It had far less to do with rescuing Jack and Carly from the sea, than it did to keeping his guard up around Olivia. It was exhausting pretending that he didn't like her a lot more than he should.

The way she'd leapt into the sea without a thought for her own safety was so typical of her. She obviously wasn't the strongest swimmer in the world, but she wasn't capable of standing by and doing nothing when someone was in trouble. He'd seen it with her at the school too. She was in early every day she was working and stayed late every night to make sure her lessons gave every child something to look forward to.

He might have been the one to introduce Hugo, the school farm cat, to Connor, but Olivia had been the one to really transform the little boy. She'd got him painting and making models of the cat and had found a way to really engage him. And, whenever Seth saw Connor now, he seemed to have a permanent smile on his face.

"Thanks again for today, mate. You and Liv did a great job." Ben got back to the flat about an hour after Seth, having gone for a final drink on his own with Ellie. By the time he got back, Seth was nursing a cup of coffee that was almost as black as his mood.

"No problem."

"Are you okay? You look the same as you did that day you came back with Joey, like someone's really hacked you off."

"I'm just annoyed with myself. I know I've got to keep Olivia in the friend zone, it's not fair to either of us, otherwise. But there's just something about her, do you know what I mean?"

"I do, and it's pretty obvious to everyone else that there's something between the pair of you, too. Even Ellie's coming around to the idea that it might do Liv some good to go out with you after what she went through with Josh, as long as you're straight up with her."

"So I'm the rebound guy?"

"You wouldn't have to be if you weren't going to San Diego."

"But I am." Seth sighed.

"You don't sound nearly as excited about the job lately. When you first arrived it was all you could talk about."

"I know, I was almost as big a bore about that as you were about the wedding." Seth laughed and ducked his head, as Ben hurled a cushion at him. "I'm only joking and I was single-minded about the job, I know. But since I've been working at the school, making new friends and then rescuing Joey, it doesn't seem to have the same exclusive appeal. I can imagine another type of life now."

"With Liv?"

"It's a bit early for that! And I'm not about to give up on the chance of the job I've worked so hard for, because of someone I've just met." Seth laughed again. "I know you're a certified romantic now, Ben, but I'd just like the chance to take her out and really get to know her before I leave for San Diego."

"Ask her then. Ellie's given you the green light after all."

"That's all well and good, but getting the green light from Olivia is the biggest challenge. I know how much she's been hurt in the past."

"Well, you'll never know unless you ask her. What have you got to lose?"

"Nothing I suppose." Seth stared into the blackness of his coffee cup. If that was true, then how come the stakes felt so high?

Chapter Eleven

The rest of the hen and stag party had gone, for the most part, without a hitch, after the drama of rescuing Jack and Carly. But towards the end of the party, Daisy had announced that the baby was on its way and, of course, that put the spotlight back on her. By the time her husband called later to say that the hospital had released her, and it had been a false alarm, the party had all but broken up. Seth had announced he was heading home too, so that Ben and Ellie could have a quiet drink on their own. If Olivia was honest, she'd been glad. Exhausted by the events of the day, her cosy bedroom back at the farmhouse had been more appealing than ever.

The week after the party, Olivia had swapped some sessions at the summer camp with one of the other staff, so that she could leave Kent on Wednesday afternoon to go and visit her parents in Yorkshire. It meant her usual schedule was moved around and so she barely saw Seth. There were no events at Channel View Farm, apart from a small wedding on the Saturday and Ellie had said they could easily manage without her, as long as she was back for the Sheep Grand National by Sunday. Ellie had arranged for tee-shirts to be printed and she wanted as many staff there as possible to advertise the farm as an event venue. Despite Ellie's best attempts to brush off her worries, she'd eventually confessed, over a late-night drink when neither of them could sleep, that the farm's finances often kept her awake at night. It was a new business and it was going to take a while to get on its feet, but unless they got some regular bookings over the winter months, she couldn't see how it was going to survive. But Ellie was desperate to make a success of things and do her great aunt's legacy proud. Olivia wished she knew how to help, but business and marketing were way outside her area of expertise. So, other than the offer of financial help that had already been rejected, all Olivia could do was be there to listen and offer hopeful platitudes that everything was going to be okay. But when she'd found Ellie with her head in her hands, the day before she'd left for Yorkshire - because the farm had missed out on the contract to host the local rotary club's monthly get togethers over the winter - Olivia was more determined than ever to find a way to persuade Ellie to take up her offer of investing in the farm. She'd downloaded a business plan, so she could show Ellie it wasn't just charity. The farm had so much potential and she knew Ellie could make it work, she just had to convince her that she'd be doing Olivia a favour letting her invest. There was no way she could stand by and watch her friend wear herself out with worry.

Karen had insisted that Olivia borrow her car to drive up to Yorkshire and, having left straight after summer camp finished at three o'clock, it was almost ten in the evening by the time she reached her parent's house in Yorkshire. Not wanting to disturb Jamie, one of the young boys her parents were fostering and whose sleep patterns were erratic at the best of times, Olivia had exchanged whispered greetings and hugs with her parents. So, it wasn't until the next day, while her dad was on the school run with Jamie and the other children they were fostering, that she had the chance to talk to her mum properly. Without Gerald to wake her with his morning braying, she'd slept in until almost nine and had come down to find her mother had laid on a breakfast fit for a five-star hotel.

"Thanks Mum." She kissed Janet on the cheek and was enveloped in another hug, the smell of warm bread filling the air and clinging to her mother's skin. "You'll be giving Karen a run for her money at this rate."

"As if I wasn't going to give my daughter a proper welcome home breakfast, especially as we couldn't welcome you properly last night." She smiled and gave a small shrug. "Anyway, Jamie won't eat anything I cook. The poor little soul got used to eating whatever he could find when he was with his mum. She had no idea how to look after him properly, but now he can't seem to adjust. At first all he'd want were biscuits and dry cereal straight from the packet. We've made progress, he'll eat pizza now and chicken nuggets, he even tried sausages last week. But the only vaguely healthy thing he'll eat is baked beans, although he even prefers those cold – straight from the tin. But he has a fruit smoothie for breakfast, with his dried cereal of course, and another one when he gets in from school. That way we do at least make sure he gets his five a day."

"I bet being with you and Dad is making more difference to him than you'll ever know." Olivia squeezed her mum's hand, across the kitchen table, as they sat down opposite each other. "I had the best childhood I could have wished for and now Jamie will have that too. Coming home was all I could think about when I was in Australia."

"Why didn't you come back sooner, when things with Josh went wrong?" Her parents knew what had happened but, like Karen and Ellie, her mother was obviously still struggling with Olivia's decision to stay on once she knew Josh was getting married.

"At least part of it was because I didn't want to let everyone back here down. I'd gone over there with this promise of a great new life, and to slink back six months later would have felt even more of a failure than staying on and being thoroughly miserable."

"You could never be a failure in our eyes, you know how proud Dad and I are of you." Olivia couldn't help but smile at the unnecessary words. Even in the dimly lit hallway the night before, she'd been able to make out the pictures on both walls. One side had pictures of all of the children her parents had fostered. The other was covered in pictures of Olivia, depicting everything she'd ever achieved, from getting her ten metres swimming badge at the age of eight, to graduating from university and beyond. There was no denying her parents' pride. But looking at the happy faces of the children her parents fostered, she was bursting with pride for them too. "I'd hate for you to think we're not here for you or to feel pushed out because we're fostering. You know how much we love you, don't you?"

"I know Mum and I feel the same about you and I'm so proud of you both. It's amazing what you're doing here."

"Not amazing, maybe, but it does feel like we're making a difference. Just like you do with the children you work with. How's the summer camp going?"

"It's good. There's even a chance they might keep me on afterwards. They always offer free places to some children each year with additional learning needs and the head teacher wants to get more specialist support in. Now he's just waiting for a decision from the trustees about whether he can offer me a permanent post."

"That's brilliant, darling." Her mother smiled again, but there was a slightly strained look to her face. "Although I have to admit that part of me was hoping you might look for a job a bit nearer here. Things are starting to settle a bit with Jamie and I couldn't help hoping that after all that time away you'd eventually settle a bit nearer to us."

"I'll get lovely long holidays if I get the job in Kent, so I can come up and spend quality time with you and Dad, and help you out with the children. It can be the best of both worlds." Then Olivia said the one thing she knew would reassure her mother and take away some of the guilt she was clearly feeling about devoting so much of her time and energy to fostering. "And the best part is that I'll have Karen and Ellie looking out for me, so that's almost as good as being with you and Dad. Karen's husband, Alan, is great too - I've never seen her so happy."

"I know and I'm so sorry that we didn't get to their wedding and that we won't make it down for Ellie and Ben's wedding either, but with Jamie still a bit unsettled, we just can't leave him with another carer yet."

"They understand Mum, but Ellie said you're all more than welcome to stay at the farm when things are better. They inherited her great-aunt's animals when she left them the place, so even though it's mostly used as a wedding venue now, the kids would still love it there."

"I'm so glad Ellie and Karen are happy. They deserve it." Her mum hesitated for a moment, as if she was wrestling with saying something, but in the end, she couldn't stop herself. "So, what about you? Any romance on the cards since you've been back?"

"Mum!" Olivia sliced the end off from the loaf of fresh baked bread in front of her, glad that her mother couldn't read the expression on her face. "That's the last thing on my mind at the moment, I just want to get a job, get settled and feel like me again. But if it's any consolation, I'm really happy just to be home."

"That's the important thing." Her mum was right, it was the most important thing, and she didn't feel like talking about Seth. What was there to say anyway? He'd be gone in just over a fortnight, so there was no point even mentioning him.

****

After a relatively easy drive back down to Kent on Saturday afternoon, and a few late starts to the day when she was at her parents' house, Olivia was up early on Sunday to help Ellie with the animals before they headed up to Julian and Caroline's farm, for the Sheep Grand National. The event had been getting bigger over the years and since it had been the hosts' daughter, Maisie, who'd insisted that Ellie rescue Holly, Olivia felt strangely nervous about her first ever sheep race.

"You do know that Holly has absolutely no chance of winning this race, don't you?" Olivia said, after she and Ellie loaded the sheep into the trailer and set off for Julian's farm. Ben, Alan and Karen had already gone on ahead to help set up. This year, the press were coming from all across Kent and there was even a regional news crew coming down to film a small segment. What had started off a few years before as an event for just a few locals in Kelsea Bay was now attracting people from the rest of the county and beyond.

"Well that's sort of the point. I'm hoping Betsy might win and then if Holly does her little comedy trot to come in last place, we should get a mention in the papers and that might drum up a bit more business." Ellie sighed. "I know it's a long shot, but we've spent a small fortune on traditional advertising and loads of time posting stuff on social media, but we really need all the help we can get to spread the word about the farm out there."

"So, all this training you've had me doing, was that more for my benefit?" Olivia laughed.

"Absolutely!" Ellie was smiling properly now, the worries about the farm temporarily forgotten. "Although I was hoping that it might at least make the sheep run in the right direction, because they won't be on lead ropes today, they'll be running in roped off lanes with just the lure of sheep nuts to get them to the end."

"That's usually enough and I don't think they'll need a lot of coercing to take part. They haven't actually got to jump over anything thing, then?"

"No, thank goodness, because that would definitely rule Holly out! I'm not sure why they call it the Grand National rather than the Derby or something else, but I suppose it's just got more of a ring to it. When we moved to the farm and I first heard about it, I did wonder if it was cruel. But the sheep seem to love it and the extra food of course! It raises a lot of money for charity, too."

"Are the rest of Ben's family coming up to watch the race?" She wanted to ask if Seth would be there, but she was hoping Ellie might mention him without her having to.

"No, it's not really Daisy's thing and she's resting a lot at the moment, apparently, so Ben's mum and dad are running the deli and restaurant without her."

"I like Daisy more than I thought I would at first, even if she does like to make sure she's centre of attention whenever possible."

"I've got to say that's probably your fault." Ellie laughed at the expression that must have crossed Olivia's face. "And I'm guessing she probably likes you a lot more than she expected to as well."

"Okay, I think that's going to need an explanation."

"Daisy was in love with Seth for years, according to Ben, but she was always a bit too high maintenance for him and she got worse than ever whenever he was around, desperately trying to get his attention."

"I can see that happening, but what's it got to do with me?"

"Ben said Daisy calmed down a lot when she met Nathan and, on the whole, she acts almost normally around Seth now. But, when she met you, it was like she slipped right back into trying to get Seth to notice her." Ellie was concentrating on the road as the lanes got narrower, so it was hard for Olivia to tell if she thought it was ridiculous too.

"I still don't get where I come into this, it's not like Seth and I are seeing each other."

"No, but you both want to. That much is obvious, even to someone like Daisy who generally only notices how she's feeling."

"I like him, but that's all there is to it." She was glad that Ellie was still concentrating on the road, as the half-truth of what she was saying would probably have been written all over her face.

"I've known you nearly my whole life, Liv, so there's no point even trying to play it cool with me. It was pretty obvious even before I saw you kissing on the boat."

"That was just relief that neither of us had drowned." Olivia sighed, wishing it was easier. "There's no point anyway, he's going to America in fifteen days."

"That's very precise, almost as if you've got it engraved on your heart!" Ellie nudged her arm. "I know I said he wasn't right for you, and that him going away would make you two dating a disaster anyway, but watching the two of you over the last month or so has changed my mind and I think it's worth the risk. Yes, he's going away, but it's only a year's contract. He might well come back when it's over and I just don't think either of you should miss the chance to say how you feel before he goes."

"Sometimes you can be really annoying when you're convinced you're right about something, do you know that?" Olivia pulled a face. "But I just don't know if I can. What if he's not as interested in me as you all seem to think he is?"

"I'd bet my last pound on it, in fact I might have to if things carry on the way they are with the winter bookings!"

"Why don't we make it a wager then? If Holly comes last, I have to tell Seth that Daisy is right."

"And if she comes anywhere but last?"

"They you've got to go and see a circus, complete with scary clowns."

"It's a bet! And you know I hate circuses, so that tells you how much I want you and Seth to give each other a chance."

"It's a noble sacrifice, my friend." Olivia laughed, as they began bumping down the rough track towards Coppergate farm, still not sure whether she wanted Holly to finish last or not. Fate – in the form of a very clumsy sheep – would just have to decide.

****

By the time they lined up at the start over an hour and a half later, Olivia was back to feeling strangely nervous. Holly and Betsy were wearing little blankets, emblazoned with the words *Channel View Farm* that Karen had hand embroidered. It suddenly felt as if the race really mattered and she couldn't put her finger on why. There was the prospect of having to tell Seth how she felt about him, but it was more than that; an uneasy feeling that this *just-for-the-fun-of-it* race was a make or break moment in more ways than one.

There were twelve sheep racing and there'd already been a fancy-dress contest for the best dressed owner, which Julian's daughter had won, in a sheep-dog costume that was completely fitting for the event. Then there'd been a best-in-show contest for the racing sheep, and a few others who'd been brought up to the farm just for that. Ben and Seth, presumably because they worked with animals, had been asked to judge it. So, if Holly lost, there'd be no putting off Olivia's end of the bet and now all that remained was the big race.

Olivia put Holly into her lane, the sheep blinking and immediately putting her head down to graze, even though the grass had been cut short especially for the race. It wasn't an auspicious start.

"Go on girl, you can do it." Olivia laughed to herself, as she noticed the other handlers giving their sheep similar encouragement. Anyone would have thought the country air had gone to their heads

"I'm going to count down from three and then release the rope that's holding them back, so if you give your sheep a pat on the behind at the same time, it should get them moving."

Julian stood on a platform made from bales of hay stacked by the starting line. "Three, two, one. We're off!"

The recent dry weather meant there was a cloud of dust as the sheep set off, racing towards the sound of children rattling buckets of sheep nuts at the finishing line. All except Holly that was. When the dust cleared, she was still standing exactly where she'd started, scuffing her lips against the ground, desperately trying to pull up some of the closely cut grass.

"Why isn't she moving?" Julian called across to Olivia, who shrugged her shoulders.

"No idea."

"Maybe she's deaf, as well as a bit lopsided." Caroline, Julian's wife, walked over to stand next to Olivia. "She doesn't seem to be reacting to the sound of the sheep nuts in the bucket, that usually has them all running."

"Can sheep even be deaf?" Olivia had heard it all now. A Sheep Grand National was unusual enough, but a hard-of-hearing sheep? "I thought she'd just charge after the other sheep anyway, even if she couldn't hear. Isn't that what they do, herd?"

"Holly has always done her own thing." Caroline smiled. "She was rejected by her mother and we bottle fed her and some others. Of course, she ended up being Maisie's favourite and she treated her more like a dog than a sheep. Then when we told her we couldn't keep her on the farm because of her limp, Maisie was really upset. It was only Ellie taking her in that calmed Maisie down, but she'd only been there a few weeks before she ended up with the name Holly Houdini. She clearly doesn't want to race and Holly only does what she wants to!" As Caroline spoke, a cheer went up to signal that the winner had finished the race.

"Maybe I can try to tempt her with some sheep nuts and walk backwards until we get to the finish line." It didn't matter whether Holly finished, but Olivia wanted her to. She was going to come last now and she'd have to honour her bet, but getting Holly to the finish line would at least put that off for a bit.

"Here you go." Caroline handed Olivia a bucket of sheep nuts and she ducked under the rope to stand in front of Holly.

"Come on girl." Shaking the bucket, Holly moved a couple of steps forward, but, when she wasn't given any nuts, she dropped her head again and pulled at the grass. "And they say sheep are stupid!" Olivia put a few sheep nuts into one hand and rattled the bucket again with the other. Holly took the offered nuts and moved another couple of steps forward, as Olivia began walking backwards. She repeated the process, giving Holly a small handful of nuts each time, all the way to the finish line, where Holly got an even bigger cheer than the winner did. A journalist from the local paper came over to take photos of Holly and Betsy, who much to Ellie's delight had won the race, and to interview Ellie and Olivia. Afterwards everyone seemed to want their photograph taken with Holly, and it was almost half an hour before Olivia had the chance to speak to Ellie.

"Well, Holly certainly made her presence felt!"

"It's brilliant and that guy from the local paper took down some details about the farm which he said he'd try to mention in his article. You never know, it might even get us a booking or two." Ellie patted Holly's neck as she spoke and Olivia silently prayed that her friend was right. She deserved some luck.

"Caroline said she thought Holly might be deaf. Can sheep even be deaf?"

"I don't know, I suppose so." Ellie looked up. "Ben's heading this way with Seth, so I'll ask him to check her out just in case. Then you and Seth can have a chat. You've got something to say to him, after all!" Ellie laughed, she wasn't going to let Olivia get away with it.

"Thanks." She watched Ellie walk towards Ben, with Betsy and Holly who were both now back on their lead ropes.

"That was nothing short of a miracle, getting Holly to the finish line." Seth's eyes crinkled in the corners when he smiled.

"I'm not sure about a miracle, but it was hard work!"

"Maybe you should let me take you out for dinner, to get your energy levels back up?"

"You don't mind being seen out with a loser?"

"That's the last thing anyone could call you, even if you did finish last today." Seth kissed her lightly on the lips and so quickly that it was almost over before she realised what he'd done. "I would apologise again, but I'm not sorry. I keep saying that, don't I? And I keep kissing you. Maybe I'm as slow on the uptake as Holly, but I'm hoping it might be third time lucky."

"If you were staying I'd definitely want to see where this might go, but we've only got a couple of weeks." It was as close as she could bring herself to keeping her promise to Ellie.

"Or you could say we've wasted too much time already."

"You're right." Maybe the country air *had* gone to her head after all, but she wanted to spend time with him before he left. It might be madness to date someone moving half way around the world in a couple of weeks, but he'd echoed her exact thoughts from the day of the boat trip. Time was running out fast, it was now or never.

"So, dinner then?"

"That would be lovely." She looked down at her jeans, which were covered in flecks of half-chewed sheep nuts. "Although I might have to change first!"

Chapter Twelve

Olivia's dinner with Seth was the best first date she'd ever had. They'd got to know each other as friends over the month or so before she finally agreed to go out with him, and they had plenty to talk about, between their jobs at the summer camp, Ellie and Ben's forthcoming wedding and Holly's antics at the Sheep Grand National. So there were no awkward silences. It was just the first of five dates they managed to squeeze in during the last week of summer camp. Ellie had been busy too, but really disappointed that the news article about the sheep race hadn't mentioned the farm and the photographs they'd used all but obscured the name on Holly and Betsy's blankets. She'd shrugged it off, after some comforting words from Karen and Alan, but Olivia knew that help from her parents was the last thing Ellie wanted to resort to and she couldn't help but worry about her friend. Not knowing what else to do to help, she'd contacted an ex-colleague from the first school she'd worked at in London, Marcus, who'd given up teaching to manage the band his brother was in and run their social media accounts. Whether he could suggest anything that might make the farm more noticeable amongst all the other advertising online, Olivia didn't know, but at least he'd offered to take a look. Winter might seem a long way off when yet another glorious day on the Kent coast stretched out in front of them, but for a struggling business it would come all too soon.

It was a great relief when the sun was out again on the day of the party to mark the end of the summer camp. The Sheep Grand National had raised over eighteen hundred pounds and Peter Coleman had arranged for sweatshirts to be printed for all the children who'd attended the summer camp, as well as booking a magician and a face painter. A big barbeque had already been laid on and the outdoor pool would be open for anyone who wanted to use it. There was still over half the money left to send to St Josephine's, so a group of children in Africa would start the next term with new stationery and other equipment, because of a quirky little sheep race in the heart of the English countryside.

"You look lovely today." Seth was already at the school when she arrived to help hang out the bunting and set up the chairs and tables. The children's families were attending the event too, so a lot of the staff had volunteered to go in early.

"I'm not sure if I should be offended by that, do I look terrible most of the time then?" She was teasing him, but two could play at that game.

"Well, I wouldn't say terrible..." He laughed as she raised her eyebrows. "You always look lovely, Liv, but you look even better than usual today."

"Hmm, that's more like it." She could be herself with Seth and it was only when she thought about the days slipping past that her mood dipped. But, most of the time, she pushed that thought back down again. She still didn't know whether she had a permanent job at the school and, if she let herself, she could worry about that too, as well as Ellie's fears about keeping the farm afloat. All of that could spoil her last day at summer camp. She wanted to make the most of being with the children who'd made her summer one she'd never forget, and worrying about everything else was pointless. She could deal with that on another day and sign up to some teaching agencies if she needed to. She just had to take the same approach to Seth leaving. Constantly thinking about that would just spoil what they had. Maybe he'd come into her life to remind her that there were good men out there, after wasting so much time on someone like Josh. Whatever the reason, she was glad he had.

"Have you seen how Joey is with the donkeys since Ellie put him in their paddock?" It made her laugh just thinking about it.

"Yes! He tries to play with them like he's a puppy or something, but poor old Gerald didn't look too amused."

"Thank goodness you went a different way and ran past him that day. I can't bear to think what would have happened to him otherwise."

"It's been a team effort from the four of us, to get him well again. Although Alan has definitely had a hand in feeding him up. I keep catching him every time I'm up there, talking to Joey and turning up with slices of apple or carrots." Seth turned and smiled at her again, as they finally finished putting out the last of the tables and chairs. The sun was reflecting on the water in the pool and the tiles that lined it, making it a very inviting shade of blue. "What has Peter put you in charge of today?"

"I'm doing an art activity. He's got some huge white canvases and washable paint in some fantastic colours, so I'm just going to let the kids do what they want with it – hand prints, foot prints or just flicking it on with a brush. I want to get as many of the children to take part as I can, Peter said he'll get prints made from canvases for the families and put the others up in the Great Hall for everyone to enjoy. I love the way this school embraces children of all abilities and it's why I was really hoping I might get a job offer."

"You still might. But like we've said before, sometimes things happen for a reason and, who knows, you might even get a better offer."

"I'm not quite sure there is a better teaching job than working here, at least not in my experience. It feels a bit like the eleventh hour, but I'll keep hoping they're going to offer me the job until I know for sure that it's not going to happen." Olivia shrugged, pushing the worry down again. "What about you, what's Peter got you doing?"

"Would you believe the barbecue?"

"I would actually! I'd say you've got off lightly, but it looks like it's going to be really hot today, so I'd rather get covered in paint and have the excuse to jump into the pool afterwards to wash off."

"Do you know what I'm looking forward to most today?"

"No, what?" She expected him to say 'going home' or having access to as many hotdogs and burgers as he could eat, but he didn't.

"Walking back to the farm with you afterwards." He smiled. "From that first time we walked back together, after Bert and Hetty's little dog got hit by the car and it was just so easy between us, I wanted to get to know you better."

"And now you have, but you still want to spend time with me?" She was teasing him again, but this time he didn't join in.

"More than ever. In fact..." Whatever it was he'd been about to say was lost, as Peter Coleman arrived and asked if anyone could recommend an emergency plumber who could come out on short notice. There was a leak in the school kitchens, where the rest of the food was being prepared, and despite his best efforts, the caretaker hadn't been able to sort it out.

The rest of the day passed in a rush of activity and Olivia had tears in her eyes when some of the children presented her with a huge box of chocolates and a card with *'No 1 teacher'* emblazoned on the front. But the best moment of the day came when Connor, who'd hated the summer camp at first, admitted he didn't want to leave.

"You must be looking forward to getting home and giving Jasper a hug?" Olivia crouched down by the little boy, who was frowning hard.

"I am, but it's like when I came here, and now it's Hugo I'm going to miss and I might not even get a chance to see him again." He stroked the cat, who was stretched out on his lap enjoying the afternoon sunshine.

"You can see him next year when you come back to camp."

"A year's forever, though." For a boy of Connor's age, it must seem that way.

"What about if you wrote to Hugo to let him know what you've been up to and to find out how he is. You might even be able to have some photos of him."

"Cats can't write letters!"

"I know, but I'm sure one of the teaching assistants would write the letters to let you know what antics Hugo has been up to." Olivia just hoped she wasn't making promises that she wouldn't be in a position to keep if she didn't get the job. "Did you hear what Hugo did today?"

"Yes!" Connor laughed, his face completely changing as a result. "He knocked a whole tray of sandwiches on the floor just to get the ham out!"

"That's right, but I think it's probably Seth's fault for getting him addicted to ham, don't you?"

"Definitely." Connor looked down at his lap and then said shyly, "it's not just Hugo I'll miss, I'll miss our art lessons too."

"Well I'm relying on you to get everyone else started with painting the big canvases later."

"Okay and will you be teaching at next year's summer camp?"

"I hope so." Olivia bent down and stroked the cat's head, as it lazily opened one eye, before stretching out again. Hugo definitely had the right attitude to life.

****

She'd hardly had the chance to speak to Seth all day until they'd finally cleared everything away at the end of the party.

"So, was running the barbeque as tiring as it looked?"

"Absolutely." Seth nodded his head. "Remind me never to consider a career in catering."

She didn't tell him that she wished he would, if it meant that he'd stay on in Kelsea Bay. He was about to realise his dream and she could hardly compete with that, but something had been on her mind all day. "This morning, when Peter interrupted us, what were you going to say?"

“Ah, there you are!” Peter had a typical head teacher’s tone, his voice carrying across the quadrangle where they were standing. If his plan had been to interrupt them every time they had a moment together, his timing was impeccable.

“Sorry.” She mumbled the apology to Seth, as she turned to face Peter.

“I thought I might have missed you.” Peter was puffing hard as if he’d been running.

“We’ve just finished clearing up, so we were about to head off.” She just hoped Peter hadn’t found another job for them to do before they left. She wanted to spend at least some of the evening with Seth.

“I’m so glad I caught you, because I wanted to tell you in person that I’ve just had a call from the Chair of the Trustees to say that they’ve approved the funding for your post. If you still want it, we’d like to offer you a full-time job from next month when the children come back for the autumn term.”

“That’s amazing, thank you!”

“We’re delighted to have you join us. I’ll email you all the details tonight, but I wanted you to know straight away.” Peter smiled. “Thanks again to you both for all your work this summer, we’ll miss you Seth.”

“Thank you, Peter. I’ll miss everyone too.” Seth shook Peter’s hand.

“Enjoy your evening, both of you. I’m off for a well-earned cup of tea now and a slice of Mrs Coleman’s carrot cake. I haven’t had time to grab a morsel today.” Peter patted his well-rounded stomach. “Although no doubt she’ll say that will do me good for once.” He turned with a final wave, the prospect of cake sending him puffing in the opposite direction.

“Congratulations!” Seth took her hand and she really wanted to kiss him, but there were still some of the other staff around and the last thing she wanted to do was to look unprofessional in front of her new colleagues.

"Thank you, I'm so relieved."

"I always knew they wouldn't want to let you go." There was a hint of wistfulness in his voice and Olivia kept her hand in his as they finally headed out of the school gates.

"So maybe third time lucky again, what was it you wanted to say to me earlier?"

"It doesn't matter, now, I just want to talk about your good news." Seth pulled her closer to his side as they began the walk up the hill towards the farm. True to his word, they talked nonstop about her new job and her plans for making a permanent home in Kelsea Bay. Excited as she was about the news, Olivia couldn't help wishing Seth would tell her what it was he'd wanted to say; but now she'd probably never know.

****

"We're very much looking forward to having you join us, Seth." Professor Glass had a New York accent and Seth knew from Googling his new colleagues that she'd worked in research centres all across America, and had a stint in Africa before heading up the team in San Diego. He also knew what she looked like, with long blonde hair and sky blue eyes. But it didn't matter if every woman in San Diego was beautiful; none of them would be Olivia.

"I'm looking forward to it too." Seth forced some inflection into his voice, so that it didn't sound as monotone coming out of his mouth as it did in his head. This wasn't supposed to happen. He'd always found it easy to end relationships, too easy perhaps; but he hadn't even had the chance to ask Olivia if she'd think about coming to San Diego with him. Peter Coleman had managed to throw off his carefully planned speech. It would have been much easier to sell the appeal of taking a chance on working in America for a while, if she hadn't just been offered the job she'd been so desperate to get.

"Have you got any questions about how things are going to work when you get out here?"

"Not really, I just wanted to ask about holidays again?"

"You'll get six weeks in the time you're here, but we need a team of staff to cover the core operations of the research centre at all times, of course. So you'll have to liaise with the rest of the team to schedule in your vacations." Some of the warmth had left the Professor's voice. She clearly wasn't impressed that his only question was about when he could take leave. But he had a reason to come back now. He'd made a commitment to Joey and he tried not to feel guilty about using the horse as an excuse, when the main reason he wanted to come home was Olivia. Maybe then they could find a way to keep things going until he decided if he wanted to settle in America for good. If they still felt the same about each other after the year was up, asking her to move out there with him would seem less ridiculous than it did after two weeks.

"I'm sorry, I know it doesn't seem like an important question, but you've covered all the other points so well in our previous discussions and I've rescued a horse that I'm keeping in livery on my friend's farm. He was in a pretty bad way, so I'm just hoping to fly back for a week every now and then to check on his progress in person."

"Well that's what we want to hear from our team, that animals are the centre of their lives! They need to be for the commitment we're after."

"Oh they're definitely the most important thing to me and, as I said, I really can't wait to start." As Seth ended the call he shook his head, wondering if he'd just told his new boss an outright lie. Working with animals had been his priority for so long, but something had changed. And the timing couldn't have been worse.

Chapter Thirteen

"Are you nervous?" Olivia watched Ellie applying lipstick in the mirror in front of her.

"A bit, but not nearly as much as I thought I would be." Ellie turned to look at her. "Because I know marrying Ben is the right thing to do and I can't wait to start our life together."

"I'm going to move out, as soon as I can find a flat to rent."

"That's not what I meant and you know it!" Ellie rolled her eyes. "You can stay here as long as you like, it's a big house and you can almost have your own wing if you want it. It's not us who think you'll be in the way, so you don't have to hide in your bedroom!"

"I know, but you've just said it; you can't wait to start your new life with Ben and you need some time on your own."

"Just promise me you won't move too far away."

"I'd like to stay in Kelsea Bay, if I can." She didn't tell Ellie she'd already looked at a couple of flats. Ben had offered to rent her the flat above his surgery, but it was at the far end of the High Street and she'd just got used to the quiet of the farm, so she didn't want to move right into the centre of things again just yet. The week between the summer camp party and the wedding had gone far too quickly, but she'd somehow managed to fit in registering with an estate agent and viewing two possible places to rent. The first one was a non-starter, it was a basement flat with so little natural sunlight that all the lamps had been blazing when she'd viewed it and it had still left her feeling miserable. The second flat was lovely, with big sash windows in the lounge and, if she stood on her tiptoes with her head on a very unnatural angle, she could just get a glimpse of the sea. It was also in a quiet road, opposite a piece of woodland, that reminded her of The Copse where she and Ellie had lived as children.

"We'll make that the deal then, you don't leave Channel View Farm until you've found somewhere in Kelsea Bay to rent and don't worry, I wouldn't want to rent Ben's flat either!"

"It's a deal." As Olivia spoke, Ellie held out her arms and they hugged almost as tightly as they had when she'd left for Australia. Ellie might be getting married rather than moving ten thousand miles away, but things were changing again all the same.

"Do I look okay?" As Ellie pulled away from her, she frowned. But she couldn't seriously need to ask that question, could she? Olivia had caught her breath when she'd first seen Ellie in her wedding dress, during one of the numerous fittings. But seeing it now, with her hair and makeup done, she looked even more fantastic.

"Oh El, you look so beautiful and I suppose I should thank you for not making me wear the mint green ballerina dress you picked out when we first promised to be each other's bridesmaids!"

"You could have carried it off!"

"You're the one who could have worn anything today and looked perfect, but the fact you're wearing your grandmother's dress makes it even more special." Ellie's grandparents had flown in from Spain for the wedding to stay with Alan and Karen. And the sense of a family coming together to celebrate one of the most pivotal moments in life filled the air.

"I love the fact she was wearing this, and probably feeling the same as I am now, almost sixty years ago." It was a stunningly simple three-quarter length ivory dress, with a typical 1950s style full skirt. Ellie hadn't made many adjustments during the fittings, except for the addition of a waistband studded with rows of tiny pearls that matched the ends of the hairpins securing her hair in the soft waves which went so well with the dress. "Nan told me Aunt Hilary paid for the dress and it was part of what made the day so special for her and granddad; even though losing her fiancé in the war meant Aunt Hilary never got a wedding of her own. Knowing that part of her is here too makes it feel so right."

"All of this feels like it was meant to be. You being left the farm, meeting Ben, your mum and Alan..."

"Aunt Hilary always said there was a plan for everything that happens in life. Even when she talked about losing her fiancé, she said it made her realise her purpose was to care for animals that other people had given up on. She was never bitter, but I do worry if she was sometimes lonely."

Olivia had been about to answer, to tell Ellie that it was possible to have almost everything you'd hoped for, but to still fill an emptiness you couldn't explain. But this wasn't the time or the place. She needed to talk to someone about how she was feeling - how much she wanted Seth to stay - and she needed her best friend. But Ellie's wedding day was a time for celebration and the rest would just have to wait.

"Oh girls!" Karen suddenly burst through the door, her fascinator at a far jauntier angle than she'd probably planned. "You'll never guess what!"

"Just tell me that whatever it is, it's good news?" Ellie widened her eyes.

"The best news!" Karen was breathless and she couldn't seem to stand still.

"Sit down and get your breath back and, since it's good news, you might as well have one of these." Olivia poured Karen a glass of Bucks Fizz from the bottle on the table, which was supposed to be helping to calm Ellie's nerves but which she'd been far too terrified of getting down her dress.

"Thank you, sweetheart." Karen took a sip of the drink. "Well, I don't know where to start really."

"Just tell us what sent you running up here like a woman possessed." Ellie appeared to change her mind and poured herself a drink, holding the glass away from her body as if the contents might explode all over her at any moment.

"Well, Alan was checking the farm's email account." Karen smiled. "You know how thrilled he is about giving you away, but he's been like a cat on hot bricks all week, worrying about the speech and making sure you get the day you deserve."

"I keep telling him not to worry. He's been more of a father to me over the last year than Dad ever was and he's here for me, that's all that matters."

"I know, love, but you know what he's like when the nerves kick in. Anyway, he's been keeping busy, trying to take his mind off it and so that's why he was going through the emails this morning. There was one from *Agri-Rescue* in the in-box."

"The insurance company?" Ellie put down her drink and Olivia tried to keep up with the gist of the conversation, but she knew almost nothing about farming, and even less about agricultural insurance companies.

"That's the one, and this is the bit you're never going to believe." Karen was back up on her feet again. "They've decided to hold their regional events at venues with links to agriculture and they want to hold the London and South East region events at Channel View Farm! And the best part is that almost all the events are over the winter months so they don't clash with any of the agricultural shows, right when we've been struggling to make bookings."

"I can't believe it! You're joking?" Ellie put down her drink, shaking her head. "Are you sure they haven't got us mixed up with someone else?"

"I'm positive and it's all down to Holly and Olivia." Karen put her arm around Olivia's waist.

"But there wasn't even a mention of the farm in the local paper." Ellie picked up her glass again, clearly finding it difficult to take it all in.

"I know, but it turns out all that's old hat anyway. Apparently, some pop group uploaded a video to their website from someone else's Facebook page, of Olivia coaxing Holly to the finish line and Alan said they looped the farm in."

"I think he probably said linked, Mum." Ellie grinned, the good news finally seeming to sink in.

"Oh yes, that's it! You know me and computers, love, give me a food mixer any day! Anyway, apparently the video went viral, which he said means loads of people watched it. And somehow, someone with the clout to make those sorts of decisions at *Agri-Rescue* saw it, read a bit more about the farm on the review sites and put a proposal to us for some block bookings. There'll be between one and two events a month this winter, whilst they phase out the bookings they've made with their current venues, but after that they'll be at least one a week. Alan said the bookings for this winter will be more than enough to put the farm into the black and then next year the sky's the limit!"

"That's amazing." Now Olivia understood why Karen couldn't keep still and she couldn't stop smiling either, this was the best wedding present Ellie and Ben could get. There was no need to mention her email to Marcus, who she was almost certain was behind this, but she definitely owed him dinner next time they met.

"I didn't think this day could get any better." Ellie's eyes were brimming with tears. "But it was the one thing casting a shadow over the wedding and I thought it was too much to ask that it could come right too. As if I was being greedy asking for that, when I already had so much. But now thanks to Liv it has."

"I didn't do anything." Olivia laughed. "And I'll try not to think about how many people have seen how big my bottom looks from behind!"

"Nonsense, you're beautiful. Both my girls are." Karen put her other arm around Ellie's waist and pulled the two girls close into her sides, risking her fascinator being knocked off her head altogether. "I've always thought of you as a second daughter, Liv, and it's been such a brilliant summer, having you home, Ellie getting married, and now this. There's honestly nothing else I could ask for."

"Me neither." Ellie murmured in agreement as Karen hugged them tighter still, but Olivia didn't say anything. Ellie was right, asking for one more thing when you already had so much was greedy. But she couldn't bring herself to say there was nothing else she wanted. How could she when Seth would be gone in less than two days?

****

The wedding went perfectly and the look on Ben's face when he turned to see Ellie walking up the aisle would stay with Olivia forever. The animals hadn't been left out of the service either. Gerald, the donkey who'd brought the couple together, had been led in as ring bearer and for once he'd behaved impeccably. Olivia had turned her head, just as Ellie and Alan stopped to face the registrar, and made eye contact with Seth. How could she have been naïve enough to think he'd help her get over Josh? She was over Josh alright, but at what price? Taking Ellie's bouquet, she sat in the first row of chairs, next to Karen, who'd given up fighting the tears that had been threatening all day.

The speeches had been moving too, but it was Alan's speech about his step-daughter that had brought a lump to Olivia's throat. He said that although he'd only been her *'dad'* for a year, she and Karen had already brought a whole life time worth of happiness into his world. Seth made a few jokes in his speech, but the humour was pitched just right and there were no bawdy remarks about the bridesmaids, just the stock line that they looked beautiful. Olivia was the only grown up bridesmaid, with little Maisie, Caroline and Julian's daughter, making an adorable flower-girl. It wasn't until the dancing later in the evening that she got to talk to Seth properly.

After Ben and Ellie had their first dance, to Ed Sheeran's *'Perfect'*, other couples began to take to the dancefloor, with Alan and Karen looking like they could audition for *Strictly*. Olivia was smiling to herself, thinking about how everyone had their hidden depths, when Seth walked towards her.

"You look almost as happy as the bride."

"I was just watching Alan and Karen. I love what they've got and he clearly wants to do everything to be the man she deserves. Who'd have thought he'd be so light on his feet?"

"I know, I love it when people surprise you like that." He gave her another one of his meaningful looks. So many times it had seemed as if he wanted to say more, but he always held back. "At the risk of humiliating ourselves in comparison to Alan and Karen, do you fancy a dance?"

"I thought you'd never ask." Olivia took his hand as he led her to the dancefloor.

"I know I said it in my speech, but I wanted to tell you again how beautiful you look."

"You look pretty good yourself." Olivia leant her head against his chest, as they moved slowly together. She wanted to freeze the moment, when everything seemed right in the world. Her mother had texted that morning to tell her to wish Ellie luck for her big day and to say they'd put a deposit down on one of the mobile homes in the caravan park next to Alan's farm. It meant her parents would be able to bring the children down for lots of holidays and they'd get to see a lot more of Olivia too, now that she'd decided to settle in Kelsea Bay. She'd got her dream job; her friends were celebrating the happiest day of their lives and now she didn't need to feel torn between Yorkshire and Kent. But there was no way of freezing perfect moments, so she tried to enjoy it instead.

"You know you asked me what I was going to say, just before Peter offered you the job?" Seth pulled away from her slightly and gently tilted her chin so she had to look up at him.

"Yes, I remember." She could hardly forget when she'd played every scenario out in her mind over the past week.

"It didn't seem fair to say it at the time. In fact it doesn't seem fair to say it now, but if I don't I might spend my whole life wondering *'what if'*."

"Just say it." She clenched her hands, where they met behind his neck.

"I know it's crazy and we've only been dating two weeks, but..." Seth swallowed hard. "I was going to ask if you'd think about working in the States for a while. I had no idea it would be so difficult to leave when we've only known each other a couple of months, but I don't want to go. At least not without you."

"I don't want you to go either." It had been too much to hope that he might stay in Kelsea Bay because of her. His job was a once-in-a-lifetime research opportunity and her teaching job must look easy to replace in comparison. But she'd been here before and only a fool made the same mistake twice. "But I can't go with you and I think you know that don't you?"

"Because of the job, or Josh?"

"Both, but not because I've still got feelings for Josh. It's weird, after wasting years waiting around for him, I don't even know what that was now. But I can't give up everything again to follow someone else's dream, even though I'm going to really miss you."

"These past two months have meant a lot to me."

"Me too. We're just in the wrong place at the wrong time. And if you were staying I'd really be looking forward to what might happen next."

"I knew it was a long shot." Seth dropped his gaze and pulled her close to his chest again. That was it, neither of them able to give up their separate lives to take a chance on something so fragile and new. It was madness to even think about it, so Olivia shut her eyes tightly trying to block out the thoughts running through her head.

Ben's mother suddenly ran across the dancefloor just as the song ended, making Olivia and Seth knock into the couple next to them.

"Daisy's gone into labour!"

"What again?" Seth said the words that everyone must have been thinking and a few people laughed.

"No, it's for real this time, but we've all been on the champagne. So unless we can find someone to drive her to the hospital, we're going to have to call an ambulance – which seems like an awful waste of their time. She's flat out refusing to go in a taxi and we'd probably have to wait hours for one at this time on a Saturday night anyway." As Ben's mother spoke, a few of the people on the dancefloor looked down at their shoes. None of them keen to break off from the party to take a pregnant woman to hospital, even if they were fit to drive.

"I can do it." Olivia broke the silence and shook her head as Seth started to protest. "I was keeping an eye on Maisie all day, so I thought it was better if I stayed off the champagne."

"You're an angel!" Ben's mother flung her arms around Olivia and then almost dragged her off the dancefloor towards where Daisy was standing with her husband, Nathan; both of them looking equally terrified. This time it was definitely for real. Olivia caught a last glimpse of Seth as she left the barn. If she'd known it was going to be the last time she saw him, she'd have said goodbye properly; but she never got the chance.

****

"I've been looking for you everywhere." Ben sat down at the table beside Seth, who'd been sitting on his own since Olivia had left, after virtually begging to be the one to take Daisy to the hospital. Had contemplating going away with him been that bad? He hadn't been planning to ask her, not once she'd got the job offer from Peter Coleman, but in the end he couldn't leave without giving it a shot. Her actions had said a lot more than her words; she didn't want to go with him. In fact she couldn't wait to leave.

"Shouldn't you be dancing with your new wife?" He didn't want to talk to Ben, he might be tempted to open up and tell him how he was feeling, and the last thing he wanted was it getting back to Liv. They'd both known what they were getting into and that it was only ever going to be fleeting; so having his friends guilt trip her into agreeing to more than that, was something he wanted to avoid at all costs. Even if that meant he had no-one to talk to about it. If he hadn't already arranged for Ben's dad to take him to the airport the next day, he'd have ordered a taxi or an Uber driver to take him that night. He'd gone from not wanting to leave, to being desperate to get away, in the space of a couple of hours.

"You know I'm no dancer." Ben laughed. "Ellie's pleased that I've done my bit and she's dancing with Alan now. I reckon he's been watching *Dancing With The Stars* on You Tube again, none of the those moves are out of the *Farmer's Little Book of Ballroom Steps*."

"I'm not even going to ask if there's a book called that." Seth just about managed a smile. This was Ben's night and he wasn't going to bring it down, even if he felt as though he'd been punched in the stomach when Olivia had walked out; knowing he might not see her again for months. Maybe not at all if she decided she didn't want to see him when he came back to visit, or if she'd moved on herself by the end of the year.

"I very much doubt there's a book called that, but right now I wish there was one called *The Zoologist's Guide to Happiness*. You look like you're at a funeral!"

"I'm sorry, I thought I was hiding it." He turned to look at his friend. He was going to tell him the truth, not the whole truth, but at least enough to explain why he was looking so miserable. "It's been a great day, it really has. But I've just realised that I'm not going to see you again and that this is it, the last night I'll spend with you all for God knows how long. I'll miss you, Joey, Ellie... everyone, even Daisy. I'll probably be gone before we hear whether she's had the baby or not."

"Don't worry, I'm sure you'll hear lots about Daisy's baby. There'll be pictures all over Facebook and Instagram by the time he's ten minutes old. Or at least by the time she's had a chance to have a full makeover, so she looks perfect in the 'new mum' pictures." Ben laughed and Seth would have bet his plane ticket that his friend was right. In fact, he'd have been tempted to swap his plane ticket for some magic beans, or even some ordinary ones, if he thought that was what Olivia really wanted.

"Oh, I've no doubt I'll find out eventually."

"And what about Liv? Will you miss her?"

"Of course, but it's all of you, this place and even the school. I'll miss it all."

"Seth, just the person I was looking for!" Ellie marched across to the table having finished her dance with Alan.

"Your husband has just said the same thing."

"Yes, but for very different reasons, I suspect." Ellie narrowed her eyes and Seth wondered if he was in for a telling off. If she told him he'd been in the wrong to ask Olivia to go to San Diego with him, he didn't know if he could keep it in. He might just blurt out that it wasn't Olivia who'd been hurt this time.

"Am I in trouble?"

"In a way." Ellie sat down at the table and took hold of her husband's hand, as she looked at Seth and then back towards Ben. "Do you know what this friend of yours has gone and done?"

"No, but I've got a feeling I'm about to find out."

"Alan's just told me that he's transferred twenty thousand pounds into the farm's bank account."

"What on earth have you done that for, Seth?" Ben was frowning.

"It's just Joey's livery fees, that's all."

"For the next ten years?" Ellie shook her head. "I know the real reason you did it, Seth, and I love you for it, but we couldn't accept your help with the farm's finances even if we still needed it."

"Please don't tell me you've decided to sell up." Seth wasn't sure he could take any more bad news.

"Nothing like that and it means so much that you and Liv both offered to lend us money, Mum and Alan too, but those worries are behind us now." Ellie was smiling in a way she definitely wouldn't have been if she was being forced to sell the farm.

"I was just about to get around to telling Seth that. It was the first thing Ellie whispered to me on our way back down the aisle." Ben mirrored his wife's smile. "We've got the contract to host loads of corporate events for *Agri-Rescue* and it looks like the winter months might be even more profitable for us than the summer season now. So you can all stop trying to bail us out, even though, as Ellie said, we couldn't be more grateful for your support and generosity. But we'll be sending your money back and there's no way we're letting you pay us for looking after Joey either, it'll be our way of saying thank you."

"That's fantastic news." Seth stood up and moved around to their side of the table, hugging them both in turn. "But I'm still going to pay the going rate for Joey's livery, even if you won't accept it all in one go."

"We'll argue about that some other time." Ben sat back down with Ellie as he spoke.

"So what were you two in such deep conversation about before I came over?" Ellie looked up at Seth, raising an eyebrow that suggested she wasn't going to be fobbed off.

"I was just admitting to Ben that I was feeling a bit melancholy about tonight being my last night in Kelsea Bay, and how much I'm going to miss you all. And Joey too."

"And I was just about to tell Seth that those feelings will probably only last until the moment he feels the sun on his face when he steps off the plane in San Diego and gets so lost in all that ground-breaking research that he forgets who we even are." Ben put his arm around his wife.

"Well there is that." Seth forced another smile, knowing with almost certainty that his friend was wrong but silently praying that somehow, against all the odds, he'd turn out to be right.

Chapter Fourteen

Olivia promised she'd wait at the hospital; after she'd dropped Daisy, her husband and her mum at the maternity unit. Just in case, despite all the signs to the contrary, it turned out to be another false alarm after all. Had she agreed to drive so willingly because she didn't want to talk to Seth again, in case he made her another offer part of her didn't want to refuse? Either way, the waiting seemed preferable to returning to the farm without any definite news. As it turned out, five hours later, at 3.30 a.m., Daisy became proud mum to a little boy they decided to call Monty. After having a brief look at the baby, and grabbing a couple of photos of their brand-new nephew for Ben and Ellie, Olivia finally drove back to the farm. It was almost five in the morning by the time she climbed into bed, but sleep still wouldn't come. As difficult as saying goodbye to Seth was, she couldn't let him go without telling him how torn she was. Even if, when it came down to it, she just couldn't risk being one of those people who went through life charging from one bad decision to another. It had been a bad decision to go to Australia with Josh and an even worse one to stay there for so long. A settled life in Kelsea Bay, with a steady job, was the sensible choice and it was about time she started making those. But she wanted Seth to know that it hadn't been an easy decision and that San Diego was somewhere she'd be more than happy to visit in the school holidays. He might not want that – it might be all or nothing for him – but she couldn't let him leave without finding out.

🖂 OUTGOING TEXT: To Seth

Sorry I had to dash off without saying goodbye. Don't know if you heard, but Daisy had a gorgeous little boy called Monty, so you'll have to eat your words about it being another false alarm! I know you're off to the airport hotel this afternoon, but please don't go before I see you. There's something I need to say. Liv xx

Putting her phone on the bedside table after she'd pressed send, she wedged her head between two pillows, hoping it might block out the sunlight already creeping through the gap in the curtains and the sound of Gerald's braying when it started. Unfortunately, it did the job far better than she'd ever imagined and it was after one o'clock in the afternoon when she eventually woke up. Picking up her phone to see if Seth had replied, she scrolled through her texts and an error message flashed up on the screen notifying her that her last text, the message to Seth, had failed to send. Getting a phone signal up at the farm was hit and miss, but she'd been too tired to think about checking that the message had sent properly and now it was probably too late.

Pulling on a pair of jeans and a long-sleeved tee-shirt, she ran down the stairs two at a time, without even bothering to brush her hair.

"We wondered when you were going to wake up, sleepy head!" Ellie smiled, her new wedding band catching the sunlight as she waved her hand at Olivia.

"I'm so sorry, I wanted you two to have the lie in this morning. It's bad enough that you've got to put your honeymoon off until the end of the wedding season, without this." Olivia's head still felt heavy with sleep.

"Don't be daft! Alan told us last night that he was coming over here as soon as it got light this morning to sort all the animals out, so we haven't had to do a thing. Anyway, you deserved a lie in after becoming a stand in paramedic for the night."

"More of a taxi driver than a paramedic." Olivia didn't want to talk about Daisy, despite the events of the night before. "Is Seth coming up to the farm before he leaves?"

"He's already gone. My dad's driving him up to the airport hotel now." Ben looked at her and then furrowed his brow. "What's up?"

"I thought he might want to say goodbye. I texted him last night to tell him I wanted to speak to him before he left, but it didn't go through." She sat down at the kitchen table, all the adrenaline that had sent her running down the stairs draining out of her. It was all too little, too late.

"He was completely miserable after you left last night and he kept watching the door of the barn when anyone came in, I know he was hoping it was you every time." Ben sat down next to Ellie.

"Did something happen between you two before you left? I thought it was a bit strange, you volunteering to take Daisy to the hospital." Ellie didn't miss a thing.

"Seth asked me if I'd go to San Diego with him and I suppose I didn't know what else to say after I'd said no. I couldn't possibly go, could I? Not after Josh."

"But Seth's not Josh." Ellie gave Olivia a long look and it was as though her brain was finally kicking into gear, as the fog of oversleeping cleared. Ellie was right and it was why she needed to speak to him, to explain.

"I know, but I still can't go away with him because everything else I want is here and it's just too much of a risk to give it up again for something that has no guarantees."

"Let's face it, Liv, there are very few guarantees in life." Ellie sounded just like her mum.

"When did you get so wise? Maybe everything's a risk but going to San Diego is just *too* big a risk for me right now. I wanted to tell him I can wait, though, that I'm not in a rush to meet anyone new the moment he leaves, and that maybe we can see each other again when he comes back to visit or I could take a trip out there."

"Then, why don't you?" Ben and Ellie spoke in unison and she couldn't help laughing.

"It's obvious you two are made for each other, but it doesn't always work like that. It's too late now anyway, he's gone and maybe it's fate trying to tell me something."

"Yes, it's telling you that the mobile signal at Channel View Farm is rubbish!" Ellie was already on her feet.

"It's not too late. Get in my car and drive up to the hotel at Heathrow. At best, you'll tell him how you feel and you can have a long-distance relationship until the time is right for you to be together properly. And at worst you can have a nice dinner together and at least get the chance to say goodbye." Ellie fished her car keys off a hook on the kitchen wall.

"You really think I should go?"

"Absolutely." Ellie paused and frowned. "But can I make one suggestion?"

"Go on, I can use all the advice I can get."

"I think you should probably brush your hair first!"

****

Halfway to Heathrow the traffic started to slow gradually until it became a crawl. If it hadn't, Olivia might have made it all the way there; but as it was, it gave her too much time to think. What on earth was she doing? Driving over two hours to surprise Seth by telling him she didn't want him to go? He knew that already and what if he thought a long-distance relationship was ridiculous? It would just make them both uncomfortable; he was hardly going to want to commit to that when he was starting a new life in San Diego. The sign announcing that the Clacket Lane services were a mile ahead loomed up in front of her and even the extra twenty minutes it took for the traffic to slowly move towards it wasn't enough to change her mind. She'd go in, get a coffee, and head back down the M25 to Channel View Farm.

"Are you there yet?" She could hear the excitement in Ellie's voice from the other end of the line as she sat in the coffee shop nursing a drink that had long since gone cold. She'd considered not answering the phone when her best friend's name had flashed up, but why put off the inevitable?

"No, I'm at the services and as soon as the traffic thins out a bit, I'm coming back."

"But we agreed that speaking to Seth in person was your best option."

"No, you and Ben agreed and for a moment I thought you were right." Olivia glanced out of the window, watching cars moving in and out of the spaces in the car park outside; all of the occupants with their own lives and priorities that had nothing to do with her. Just like Seth.

"Well, I still think you should do it, but if you really don't think it's the right thing, then come home and you can finally have that glass of champagne you missed out on yesterday." There was a false brightness in Ellie's voice and Olivia knew she was disappointed. She wasn't the only one.

"Okay, hopefully I'll be home in time for dinner. I'll pick up a take away on the way back into Kelsea Bay, if it isn't completely unacceptable for me to invite myself to dinner with a couple of newlyweds?"

"Absolutely not, we're always here for you, you know that."

"Thank you." Olivia ended the call with a weird mixture of relief and that hollow feeling that had plagued her for the past few weeks. Passing a rack of wooden wall plaques at the edge of a pop-up gift shop on the way out of the service station, Olivia spotted one with a familiar message on the front that immediately reminded her of Seth, when he'd tried to reassure her about singing at the anniversary party. *This too shall pass*. She could only hope her feelings would too.

****

By the next day, Daisy had been released from hospital and she'd insisted that Ben, Ellie and Olivia visit her that same evening. Olivia couldn't for the life of her work out why. After all, she and Daisy had never exactly been what you might call friends, but Ellie said that it was probably because Daisy was so grateful to Olivia for taking her to the hospital. The cynical side of Olivia suspected it might have more to do with Daisy gloating about Seth heading off to America without even a backward glance, but nothing Ben's sister said could hurt her any more than she already had been. Maybe it was unreasonable of her to expect a goodbye text from him – or something – but he hadn't even attempted a proper goodbye. Which said a lot more than any words could have done.

"He's beautiful." Olivia leant over Monty and Daisy shot her a megawatt smile. The baby was beautiful in that way only new born babies could be, like a mini Winston Churchill with an angry, red and wrinkly face, yet more precious than anything on earth at the same time.

"He is, isn't he?" Daisy was clearly head-over-heels in love with her new son and Olivia had the feeling he'd be the making of her. The start of putting someone else first. "Nath, can you make some drinks, honey, and get Ellie and Ben to help you out?" It was more of an order than a request and the three of them filed out dutifully, leaving Olivia standing awkwardly in front of Daisy.

"So how is motherhood so far?" Olivia was hardly an expert on babies, but she had to say something to fill the silence while she willed the other three to hurry up with the drinks.

"I love it and he's being an angel. He wakes to feed and then goes straight back down again, I feel really blessed. "

"I think you are."

"It's also made me realise something. I kept wondering if I was settling for Nathan because Seth didn't want me." Daisy held up her hand. "No, let me finish. I'm sure you've worked out how I felt about him, or at least how I used to feel. Either that or Ben and Ellie will have spilled the beans."

"Does Nathan know?"

"He's got no idea, bless him." The smile that lit up Daisy's face was the most genuine one Olivia had ever seen her give. "And now he doesn't need to. I've realised that what I felt for Seth was always more about my ego than it was about him, wanting something I couldn't have made me fixate on him all the more. That *'treat her mean and keep her keen'* worked on me for years."

"We've all been there." Olivia looked at Daisy and their eyes met for a second, an understanding growing between them.

"But having Monty and seeing how Nathan has been, through the pregnancy, at the birth and since he's arrived, has made me realise once and for all what a wonderful man I married."

"There's no doubting that."

"But you and Seth..." She paused and Olivia waited for her to say that they definitely didn't have what it took. Not that she needed telling, the way he'd left told her all she needed to know. "You two, there's something there, something special. I thought he'd stay, I really did. I watched him watching you and, in all the years I've known him, I've never seen him look at a girl like that. At first, I didn't want it to be true; but now I've realised he'd never have been the right man for me, and that Nathan is the only person I want to be with, I thought I owed it to you to say it."

"You don't owe me anything, but thank you." She wasn't going to tell Daisy that it didn't matter what she thought. Seth had obviously been stringing them all along. If he'd looked at her like that, then it had been a passing moment, nothing worth giving up his dream for. And who could blame him?

"I don't want you to give up on Seth yet, not until you're a hundred percent sure that I'm wrong."

"What are you two whispering about?" Nathan came back into the room with a tray of drinks. Ellie and Ben were following in his wake, looking as if they still had no idea why they'd all been temporarily banished from the room.

"I was just telling Olivia how lucky I am to have you." Daisy reached up to take her husband's hand, while their son lay peacefully sleeping in the crook of her other arm. "Even though you've just interrupted me as I was getting to the best bit. I was about to ask Olivia if she'd consider joining Ben and Ellie as Monty's third godparent."

"Me?" Olivia had to sit down as Daisy nodded. It was as if she'd landed in some parallel universe where she and Daisy were suddenly not just confidantes but close friends. "I mean I'm flattered, but why me?"

"Because you took us to hospital on a night that was really important to you and you gave up saying goodbye to Seth to be there for me, Nathan and Monty."

"I did what anyone would have done."

"No, you didn't." Nathan smiled at her. "You made sure that the two most important people in my world were safe and this is just our way of saying thank you."

"Well in that case, I'd love to." Olivia couldn't even look at Ellie. She was sure her oldest friend would be as shocked as she was. Instead she reached down and pinched the underside of her arm. If she woke up, like in one of those dream sequences from a cheesy soap opera, and found out she'd imagined all of this, it would have surprised her less than the reality. Seth might have left without a second thought, but she was more tied to Kelsea Bay than ever now and being Monty's godmother had given her another reason to smile. Even if half of her heart had gone with Seth.

Chapter Fifteen

Olivia's first day at the school was a training day. It was just over two weeks since Seth had left for the States and, with Daisy's advice about not giving up on him ringing in her ears, she'd emailed him that first week to wish him well and give him a watered-down version of what she'd planned to tell him in person. In the end, all she'd said was that she'd love to meet up next time he was back in the UK, but stopped short of suggesting she go out there to visit him, much less that they tried to keep their fledgling relationship going on a long-distance basis. It all seemed ridiculous now even to suggest it. He hadn't replied. It had taken her the second week to stop jumping every time her phone beeped to announce the arrival of an email, but she'd come to terms with it now. Having Monty might have knocked the hard edges off Daisy, but somehow Olivia still didn't think she'd admit to being wrong about her and Seth. She'd forgiven Daisy for giving her false hope, but it was harder to forgive Seth. Okay, so they might have only been dating for a couple of weeks, but they'd built up a good friendship over the last two months and she'd thought he'd at least have the decency to reply and let her down gently. It was funny how wrong you could be about someone, but it wasn't as if it was the first time.

Everything else was going far too well for Olivia not to be grateful every day. She'd put the first month's rent and deposit down on the flat with the sash windows, and she would be picking up the keys after work. Ben had announced that he'd managed to rent his flat too, so she didn't even have to feel guilty about that. But perhaps the most satisfying thing had been the email from Josh that had arrived the night before she started her new job. He'd used a new email address, after she'd blocked his old one, and when his message came through she'd thought about deleting it without reading it, but she couldn't resist. He'd said he missed her and that he realised what a fool he'd been, but reading on she was left in no doubt about the real reason he'd got in touch. Alice had left him for someone she worked with. If that wasn't karma, then Olivia didn't know what was. She'd been tempted to contact him and tell him as much, but in the end she'd deleted his message and blocked his new email address. If she had to keep doing it until he finally realised she'd moved on, then she would.

Before Olivia had left for work, Karen had turned up at the farmhouse with a packed lunch and a tray of cakes to put in the staff room for her new colleagues. It was such a thoughtful gesture, so she couldn't bring herself to tell Karen that the staff were expected to have lunch with the children in the school's dining room. No doubt they'd enjoy the cakes anyway, even if they took them home after work; no one could bake like Karen. Ellie had insisted on meeting her after school to check out the new flat, which Olivia was moving into at the weekend. With her parents planning their first trip down to their holiday caravan before autumn set in, Kelsea Bay felt more like home every day. Even if she had woken in the night with a momentary panic that she'd missed the opportunity of a life time by turning down Seth's offer to go to San Diego with him. She was sure now she'd been right.

"Ah, Olivia, there you are. I can officially welcome you to the school!" Peter Coleman was standing outside the main entrance as she got out of her car.

"I'm really delighted to be joining the team."

"It's fantastic and, thank goodness, I've even managed to find some last-minute cover for the farm." Peter's jowls moved up and down as he chuckled. "For one minute there, I thought I was going to have to dig my wellies out and teach farm studies myself!"

"I'm sure you'd have done a great job."

"Well, put it this way, I'm mightily relieved I don't have to. I'm not as fit as I used to be." Peter raised his eyebrows, as if she might disagree. But he looked like the sort of man who spent most of his time behind a desk these days, rather than up on his feet teaching. "Actually, could I ask you to go and grab the new farm teacher, I want to get everyone in the hall in twenty minutes for a bit of a pep talk before we start the training and I've still got a hundred and one things to do before then."

"What's the new teacher's name?" Even as Olivia asked the question, Peter was disappearing through the heavy oak doors into the school.

Walking across the quadrangle towards the farm, she tried not to remember the last time she'd been there, with Seth at the end of summer camp party. He still hadn't replied to her message, so the weeks they'd spent together couldn't have meant nearly as much as she'd thought. He'd probably asked her to go to San Diego knowing that, after what had happened with Josh, she never would. It was sad to think that Seth wasn't the person she'd thought he was either, but as the days went by with no reply it was hard not to think so.

She heard a noise from the bushes, her back involuntarily stiffening. If it was the geese who'd been nesting there earlier in the summer, the first impression the new farm teacher was going to get was that she was a hysterical bird phobic or worse still someone who ran around screaming for no reason whatsoever. It was getting less and less of an issue, though. She could even look at the chickens when she let them out back at the farm now, but geese were still her nemesis.

"Hello?" Walking into the stable block, the sound of a shovel being raked across the floor was like fingernails down a blackboard. Someone was in there banking up the straw, but she couldn't see who it was in the shadows at the back of the building.

"Hello yourself." For a moment she was sure she recognised the voice, but it couldn't be. Taking another couple of steps forward, she drew level with the stable door and a figure moved out of the shadows.

"What on earth are you doing here?"

"Well, I've got to admit that wasn't quite the greeting I was hoping for!" Seth smiled.

"You're supposed to be in San Diego."

"I couldn't stay, I missed Joey Bowie too much."

"So you've given up everything you've worked for to come back and see Joey? I know he's special but come on."

"Alright, I did miss him, but not as much as I missed someone else. When I got there, all I could think about was you. Then I got your email and I knew that catching up with you when I was in the UK wasn't going to be enough. And when Ben rang me and told me about you coming half way to the airport, I knew I'd been right about us. I couldn't respond to your email, though. And I'm sorry for leaving you waiting like that, but I just wanted to be sure I could get everything sorted first. I realised as soon as I read your message how unfair it was of me to ask you to come to San Diego."

"I wanted to, I really did."

"I know you did but I also know why you couldn't come. What you said at the wedding and in your message, I finally started to get it. You just couldn't take the chance." Seth took hold of her hand across the stable door. "Brace yourself because this is about to get toe curling enough to challenge Ellie and Ben."

"Okay." As she replied, she actually felt herself tense; wanting to know what he had to say, but dreading that she might still have got it all wrong somehow.

"I've never taken a chance before, because I've never had to. I've never been in love before."

"You're in love with me?" He didn't look like he wanted the ground to swallow him up, in fact he couldn't seem to stop smiling.

"Yes, I know it sounds crazy after only a couple of weeks. But, after years of waiting for it to happen, in the end it happened so quickly it didn't even hit me until I was halfway over the Atlantic."

"Me too, except I only realised it when Ben told me you'd already left. But I just thought it was me. Rushing in, and getting it all wrong again."

"As far as I'm concerned, you get everything right." He was saying all the things she wanted to hear, but she still couldn't get her head around it.

"But you're contracted for a year."

"I was and that's why I couldn't just get straight on the next plane home, because believe me I wanted to. There's another zoologist from the Netherlands who was due to start his secondment next year. After a bit of negotiation, he managed to agree with the zoo he was at to move his secondment forward to this year instead. They've given me six months to decide if I want his place next year and, if not, they'll offer it to someone else on the list."

"It's your dream job, though. Are you sure you want to risk it all for this?" She looked around the stable block. The school farmyard could hardly compare with San Diego Zoo.

"I wanted to take a risk for you; for us. Jobs come and go, but I knew I'd always regret it if I didn't go with my gut on this and come home. If it was up to me, I'd ask Ellie to pencil us in for a date to show you how serious I am about you, before they get too booked up with *Agri-Rescue* events."

"No-one's ever done anything like this for me before but, don't worry, I'm not expecting you to promise me a wedding, or even a happy ever after. It's more than enough to know that you think I'm worth putting the rest of your life on hold for."

"You are, Liv, and I really do want what Ben and Ellie have at some point. In fact, I want to be like Bert and Hetty in the end; nagging each other like crazy after half a lifetime together, but still the most important people in the world to each other."

"If I didn't think I'd get sacked on my first day at work I'd kiss you."

"You do know Peter Coleman was in on all this, don't you?" Seth was grinning again. "He was almost as nervous as I was!"

"And what about Ben and Ellie, do they know you're back? What are they going to do about their honeymoon? They had it all planned for San Diego!"

"I think they'd have happily swapped it for Southend to see the two of us get together. And they knew all about it from the moment I landed in San Diego, but I asked them to keep it a secret to make sure I could sort everything out. Ben's even renting his flat to me, so I'll be living in Kelsea Bay too." Seth brushed a strand of hair away from her face. "And seeing as there's no one in this stable block but me, you, and a couple of ponies who've promised not to breathe a word, I am going to have to kiss you."

As Seth pulled her towards him from across the bottom half of the stable door, the final piece of her life fell into place. No-one had the right to expect everything to be perfect, and she'd had her share of ups and downs, but she was home now, surrounded by family and friends, and she'd finally found someone she knew would put her first, when she hadn't even been looking. She was grateful to Josh, too. If he hadn't shown her what she didn't want, she might never have recognised everything she had to be grateful for. And, as Karen would no doubt put it, Seth really was the icing on the cake.

THE END

Also available from Fabrian Books

Give Me Your Answer Do
By Jo Bartlett

When Ellie Chapman inherits a dilapidated farm, perched high up on the cliffs above the English Channel, it's not long before she decides to launch a wedding business. After all, with a mum whose cake baking skills rival Mary Berry's, and the perfect venue, it seems the natural choice. She might be a total novice when it comes to the first wedding, but with a bride who leaves everything until the last minute, a vengeful ex-fiancé of her own, and the world's naughtiest donkey... What could possibly go wrong?

Fabrian Books' feel good novels are heart-warming romantic stories that leave you believing a happy ever after does exist.

Resisting Mr Rochester
by Sharon Booth

Cara Truelove has always been a romantic, burying her head in books and dreaming of being swept off her feet by her very own Brontë hero. When she was a gullible teenager, she believed boyfriend Seth to be a modern-day brooding Heathcliff. Fourteen years later, when Seth has proved to be more like Homer Simpson, Cara vows never to fall in love again, and turns her back on romance for good.

Leaving Seth behind, Cara secures a job as nanny at Moreland Hall on the Yorkshire Moors, but is shocked to discover her new employer is none other than the tall, dark, and disturbingly handsome Mr Rochester.

Her resolve to be more level-headed is soon tested when strange things begin to happen at Moreland Hall. Why is Mr Rochester's mother hidden away upstairs? What are the strange noises she hears from the attic? Why is the housekeeper so reluctant to leave her on her own? And where is Mr Rochester's mysterious wife?

As events unfold, Cara knows she must keep a cool head, curb her imagination – and resist Mr Rochester at all costs. After all, one Brontë hero in a lifetime is more than enough for any woman. Two would be downright greedy.

Wouldn't it?

Escape to Sunrise Cottage
By Zara Thorne

Set in the heart of the Sussex countryside, Escape to Sunrise Cottage is a feel-good romance with a dash of mystery.

When artist Violet Brooke leaves her engagement ring on top of a Chinese wedding cabinet and runs away from the trendy apartment in London's Brick Lane, there's only one place to go – Sunrise Cottage.

All she wants is to cosy up in her rural retreat, concentrate on her painting, and forget about Jayden Fox, bad boy of the East End art scene – he's certainly forgotten about her. The last thing she needs is romance. Then handsome antique dealer Max Finch shows up in the middle of a field and the problem is, he's impossible to resist.

For Max, meeting Violet – and falling in love with her at first sight – is a turning point. His ex-wife, Sarah, has bipolar, and Max still feels partly responsible for her well-being. But Sarah has others to care for her now, and Max knows that if he is to win Violet's trust, he must put her first. Max is not the only complication in Violet's rural idyll. Before long, she's shocked to discover that somebody wants her gone from the village, and they're making sure she knows about it. But who? And why?

Is this Violet's cue to head back to London and pick up her real life? Or is Sunrise Cottage – and Max Finch – as real as it gets?

Air Guitar and Caviar
By Jackie Ladbury

Busker Dylan spends his days pulling pints in the local pub and singing on the high street, waiting for fame to call. That suits him fine, until beautiful, but frosty, air stewardess, Scarlett, tosses some coins into his hat but ignores his killer smile and his offer of pizza.

He sets out to get the girl, but Scarlett isn't in the right frame of mind to date anyone, let alone a penniless, if charming, busker boy.

Dylan's desperate for his big break, but will it bring him the happiness he longs for? And with Scarlett's past threatening to ruin her future, will Dylan be left to make sweet music all on his own?

Printed in Great Britain
by Amazon

69295896R00102